Enkel Hasamataj

The Echo
of Forgotten Corridors

Title:
The Echo of Forgotten Corridors

Author:
Enkel Hasamataj

Editors:
Dr Sarah Meehan O'Callaghan
Dr Tiziana Soverino
& Jeremy Murphy

Cover Photograph:
Kled Kapexhiu

Graphic Designer:
Kleida Maluka

ISBN 9789928393548

The spring's breeze is fluttering around the hair, collars and lapels of folks on the streets as it invites everyone to the perpetual rejuvenation dance of life while blowing more briskly and vividly after a long and frosty winter. Like a veil embroidered with pearls that have wrapped up nature, from place to place, the melted snow has shrunken and metamorphosed into small water blobs. In this blossom spree, the young prompted sprouts slightly bow their crest and thrive abundantly ever more with each passing day.

Pedestrians stroll nonchalantly on the sidewalks with a spontaneous vitality that indwells, reflecting on every smile and gaze, the multitude of bits and pieces of bluish sky and the sun's rays, whirling a harmonious waltz.

Even though the cars swarm by, astonishingly, that peculiar uproar and tangle that randomly pervades are fainter and, every so often, completely trails away, generating a void as if it were sliding loosely on ice and not whirling on wheels. A time like this takes me down my childhood memory lane, imbuing me with a startling peace that seeks to get hold of my entire being.

The evanescence of this feeling dissipates as a hand weighing down on my shoulder makes me quiver, perturbing my vernal reverie.

"Man alive! Greetings T., long time no see!" the voice of a man around his sixties gruffly spoke, wearing a pitch mary brown jacket and a grey scarf clenched around his throat.

His bag-of-spanners face and the cross-eye gaze from within deep his socket, with bulging brow ridges, racked my brain for a brief moment amid a silent duel of recollections in my mind.

"Your grasp has turned out heavier, but your soul has always been free, like an artist." I reply after I had gotten a grip on myself, and embrace him, "So many years that I have not seen you! Fifteen years, if I'm not wrong. It has been a while, hasn't it?!" I add promptly.

"Truly," he says to me, "the years have rolled away fast. You were then such a broth of a boy, and you sealed the end of each day with a new bruise or graze on your knees and body. Do you remember when I used to gather you all around and count all the bumps and scratches on your limbs? You were a bunch of nippers that I loved to bits, particularly the three or four of you, who acted the maggot and are still close to my heart. I did not expect that you would recall me after all this time."

"How can I forget the man that has helped me so many times to dodge the whipping reprimands of the adult carers?"

Sherif is the bicycle handyman who worked in our endz when I was a child. He fixed up our bicycles more than a few times, on some occasions even for free, if we didn't have enough money to pay him in order to conceal our mischief from parental concern. He was a benevolent man, without a doubt. When he used to put the inner tube in the bucket of water to spot through the bubbles where the flat tyre had the puncture, he always told us "There is no hideaway that you haven't been exploring, you rascals. Where about have you been wondering this time?"

And indeed, we roamed in all sorts of places all day long. We went by the railway and laid long nails on top of the train's rails, waiting for the wagon to slide over them and press it down to the shape of a spit.

Afterwards, we would go to the factories on the outskirts of the city. We would jump over the walls sneakily, and there we would collect chips, bearings, spheres, dice, and different pieces of bones and ivory scattered on the floor. Then, we made up all kinds of games by playing with what we found, or we would arrange the bits and pieces, building various innovative things, as in the case of ball bearings, utilizing those to make stroller carriages for our rides.

Our soft underbellies were the downhills' slops of the park at the artificial pond, which even today we still call simply the "Lake", as we whooshed through it with our bicycles.

One fine day, this bearish man of golden heart did not show up in his workshop and was lost without a trail, like salt in the sea, like a dream while napping on a summer afternoon. The word spread that he was arrested by the Central Committee since he was assumed to be an undercover mole. Others whispered hither and thither that he was killed at the border while making an attempt to flee the country. There were also those who said he had committed suicide by drowning in the sea as a result of a heartbreaking love story. Rumours boiled like tar and unfurled faster than cholera at that time when the press was centralized, and the ears-flapping were at the peak of their thriving. However, this airing of the lungs would ebb away in the gully of oblivion, only to be updated tomorrow with other "news".

I would not have recognised him if it weren't for the skin's cracks that permeated almost his entire face, crisscrossing like dry water rivulets in the desert after a storm, even more eroded and puffed up by age, as well as his jolly brown eyes, which had wearied off something of their past glow.

"I'm happy to see you in good shape." I say to him cheerfully, "You have slimmed down a bit, but considering that we thought you had gone the way of all flesh, you look fine. Anyway, you may well expect me to have the sharp memory of a young man forging away at life, but how did you recognize me after so many years? Do not tell me that I haven't changed a bit, from that tot with messy outfit, since the last time we saw each other?"

Keeping himself silent for a few seconds, he then glances at a building that stands on my right and says "Do you see that building over yonder?" pointing his index finger beyond the plaza, where we were standing, at an alley, where a two-story house with a roof deck was located.

"Yes," I answer him after I turn my head and see the building, "it is the city's photographic museum."

"Before our paths crossed, I paid a visit to take a look at how the city had been transformed during this time. The gates to enter are pretty narrow, with two side pillars that give the impression of two skyscrapers growing taller and taller. I had to slither along at those for about thirty minutes to wiggle my way in, and while I was doing that, the left shoe slipped off my foot and fell behind. Since the marble floor inside the building was clean and reflected even the tiniest details of your face, as if it were made of glass, I left it where it dropped and planned to get it back on my way out. Therefore, I decided to take off my other shoe and put it in my jacket's inner pocket."

"Well, the premises are pretty much like the city." I jump in, "Many things have changed here recently. It has become really difficult and exhausting, and you have to squeeze through to pay for a single bill at the counter."

"Yes indeed, that's how it is." he affirms, shaking his head and continuing with his story "In the hall, at the front desk, there was an old woman. With her salt-and-pepper hair tied in a knot, sitting in a rocking chair, she was diligently knitting a piece of cloth at staggering speed.

It was impressive to see her in action because she was working with six yarns at once, three in one hand and three in the other, the threads of three looms that were rotating fast and not shrinking a bit in size.

One of them was black, the other was white, while the third was transparent. So, as a consequence, it was hard to tell it apart from the others since it camouflaged itself, absorbing and reflecting the colours of the background.

The piece of cloth that she was knitting, at most a cubit wide, had the contour of a film strip, not lacking the hollow squares in its edges, by which it clings to the device. This weave was spinning wave upon wave in an opening on the wall, and it was stored in the next room. Finally, without batting an eye, the old lady addressed me

'Welcome, Sherif; I was waiting for you!'

Surprised, I asked how she knew my name since it was my first time seeing her. Without lifting her eyes, as she was calmly interlacing the threads, she confessed that she knew a lot of stuff about me. She even knew when I had learned to ribbon tie my shoes for the first time in my life.

That was her occupation, respectively, to keep a record of every important detail of the citizens that lived in the city, along with everybody else, and let them be occasional bystanders or casual passers-by. Otherwise, what benefit would the progression of the sciences and social institutions at large have?

'Maybe to ease people's burden from their everyday obligations, so they can have more time to achieve their goals and to self-develop?' I replied to her.

'Enough talking a bunch of boloney, please.' she answered me, 'The wheel was invented so many thousands of years ago as a consequence of the cyclic circulation of the seasons. And the benefit that it brought to agriculture had no comparison with anything else in the course of the civilization, and for what did you exploit it?' at this moment, she stopped moving the yarns, lifted the glasses that had slipped almost at the edge of her nose slightly, and by looking stealthily into my eyes, spoke as she waved at me her index finger 'So, tell me, for what did you use it, you wagering brutes? To multiply your enormous profits and to fight each other because of your greed for power. That is why!'

'Please, hold your water, madam.' I answered her with the first thing in my mind, 'I myself am just a petty bicycle repairman. The most significant thing that has come as a result of my fixing the tyres has been the transportation of people from home to work and back, as well as the joy felt by the kids as they drift their bicycles through the city's streets. Nevertheless, honoured lady, I am here to visit the gallery. Please tell me how much the admission tickets cost?'

As she dived again in the process of knitting, she said to me 'Just what I was saying: money has become a millstone for the grinding of the bones! The entrance is free, but first, you have to answer a riddle. It is not a conundrum like any other because it has more than one right answer, and depending on the response, you open the path for what you are seeking.'

'To tell you the truth,' I spoke to the old lady, 'I am not after anything in particular. I was wandering around and about, and to kill time, I decided to come to this museum to appease my curiosity about how the city has been transformed through the ages.'

'That's for you to decide. Anyway, the riddle goes as follows: One from the goat, and two from the stream. What the heart says, the cheek does not speak. His face has never dried. Who is it?' the elderly woman said.

The riddle was not easy at all," Sherif recounts, and his face contorts in astonishment, "and what's more, depending on the answer I was going to provide, the consequences were irreversible. The sole comfort was in the fact that the rebus had a common thread, which meant that for the same essence or feature, it was labelled with different names, as the case presented itself to the person who gave the answer. Right about when I was going to utter my response, a hand clasps me at my palm, between the thumb and index finger, pulling me deep into the gallery. It was a guiding drag in which every muscle in my body followed freely in an act of true will.

'The namelessssss', my answer echoed, as I was complying strictly with the pulling force of the mysterious hand, wherever it was carrying me. It felt more like I was being dragged while floating on water, or to be more precise as if I had been saved from drowning. Meanwhile, I tried to take a glance at the person who was pulling me, but it was as black as Newgate's knocker in there, and it was not possible to tell her apart, except some bracelets that clinked and a soft, smooth hand that was omnipotent over me."

"Sherif," I interrupt his confession for a moment, "why don't we go to a spit-and-sawdust place, where we would be comfortable and converse at ease? We can bust suds or bend our elbows with a whisky chaser. What do you think?"

He affirms by shaking his head and continues narrating his story with such passion and commitment as if he were a lad telling his adventures at some Boy Scout camp roasting potatoes over the charcoal. His spirited mimicry after every and each of his exclamations, coupled with climactic phrases, from time to time swapped to gesticulating language by moving the hands vigorously, as to give the entire possible meaning to every sentence. After swilling down a few toasts, his lips start to wobble and quiver as if he were performing in an operetta's choir.

"And as I was trying to have a better look" Sherif unravels further, "little sparks like luminescence flashlights were approaching and passing me by, radiating their neon-pale brightness in my face, as if I were travelling by train through a tunnel, and not being pulled along in the corridor of a gallery. Most varied silhouettes of drawings and photos were developed and expanded in it. In one of them, I could discern the dilapidated foundations of a ground-floor house capsized on itself and its adobe walls toppled to the ground. A little further away stood out the outlines of a skyscraper built on the ground where an ex-factory used to be. Yet in another picture, a rustic old lady, with her head covered in white chiffon and wearing loose clothing, once of a pitch black colour, but recently somewhat bleached out from extended exposure to sunlight, was sitting somewhere on a kerb on her haunches and was selling milk in a litre and a half reused plastic bottles, gazing at a customer who was getting off his posh automobile, that most likely costs as much as a small dairy factory.

Some of the images flickered, uncertain and indistinct as her golden hair shook and glittered my sight, disfiguring their images and shapes, but from those I could glimpse, one above them all got lodged into my brain. It was a picture of a man scourging his father with a leash. It was not a leash like any other, but his own nipper child, which he had grasped by the heel and was handling him as a whip, giving unrestrained blows to his father.

As the baby was nibbling the entire body with his piglet teeth, the grandfather was stroking his forelock with tenderness. I have pictured his facial features in my memory to this day as we speak."

Meanwhile, Sherif looks straight into my eyeball and keeps describing with terror written on his face "That physiognomy wasn't of a human being but of a monster, and one couldn't tell if it was crying or laughing. To this very day, I am astounded as I recall that scene.

And then, all of a sudden, we came to a halt, and the environment around us was illuminated by a blinding light. Meanwhile, the figure of the young lady who had been guiding me began to emerge from the darkness.

At this moment, she released her white, milky hand. Wasp-waisted and lissom, with blonde hair that cascaded down as a linn trailing over her round breasts, like the sunlight over a pond of rare fowls, it made me think that some shiny, wonderful fairy was standing in front of me. Smiling, she asked me with a bubbling voice 'What did you think of the exhibition, Uncle Sherif? Would you prefer to return to any of the images that have loomed in your mind?'

'It was quite impressive. And now that I have visited and seen this historic string of pearl photos of the city, I feel a different person.' I answered."

At this point, Sherif bends his body towards me, and with his eyes sparkling with excitement, he says "In a few of the photos, I could see you rowdy laddies at different times. The most recent photo was from last year, when you were celebrating a football match won by your local team in the city centre. The years that have passed have left their marks, and much has changed in your appearance, but your frolic dance as happy as a sandboy has remained the same from the times ever since I first met you. To get back to what I was saying" continues Sherif, "I told the lady that even though I couldn't flick through all the photos because most probably it was her hair that blocked my sight and made my mind go blank, in any case, it would be beneficial to my own interest to come around another day, since leaving some of the photos unseen cultivates ones curiosity to come back and look at it afresh.

'This is the reason why you are still a bachelor?' jumped in the mysterious missy, as I was about to finish my remark, 'Hehe, you like to peek incessantly through keyholes?'

'No, quite the opposite,' I answered her in sheer amazement, 'it is like, for example, when you go to a restaurant, you do not order all the dishes on the menu at the same time. So, it is the same with a lady; some things you have to promise to your soul mate for another time in order for the ember to stay aglow, the same as it was the first time you met. But this is a very personal matter that belongs only to me, and I would prefer not to discuss it any further. Please, is it not enough that an old lady hurls malevolence at me in the lobby area, but even here, I have to go through such a kind of persecution?'

'Why didn't you know that the old ladies are nothing else than toys in the devil's hands?!' she guffawed at me as she answered. So reverberating was the laugh that I had to crouch down, covering my ears with both my hands so as not to be completely deafened, while the echo of her voice kept fading away. In the blink of an eye, the walls disintegrated, and now I found myself in front of the two towering pillars at the museum entrance. I retrieved the shoe left inside the porch as I got in, took the other out of my pocket, and put them on.

Out on the main street, I happened to see you walking past and stopped by to say hello. My heart leaps to see you fine and well after so many years. I believe that a young man attractive like yourself, who likes to bat his eyelashes a mile away, should, without a doubt, be married or at least engaged?" he tells me half-jokingly with a cheeky wink after he concluded his narrative.

"Huhh, I have not yet been able to find my close-to-heart restaurant." I reply to him smiling, "For the time being, I'm content with trying my luck going out on a pull at the bean wagons. What's more, I haven't had the time to be on the prowl since I started to work as a night auditor at a hotel, whereas, during the day, I do not even know how the time slips away."

"Io and behold, from a hassle scoundrel that I once knew, now you don't have enough time even to take a deep breath and mellow out." he pokes fun at me with his debonair parlée.

"Even on those days when I am not at work, I either crash the couch or hang out with my buddies and acquaintances." I tell him.

"What about Ilir 'Hummer-forehead' and Besian 'Ricepudding'? I remember you were joined at the hip, and when you got together, there was no stone unturned in the entire neighbourhood. Do you still hang out together, or have you gone your separate ways once and for all?"

"Hammer-forehead" and "Rice-pudding" are my bosom chums' nicknames. The first belongs to Ilir, since his forehead was wide like a hummer, and the second to Besian because he has blond wavy hair and a white freckled face that made him look like a rice pudding. While my nickname was "the Eel", as I was quite agile and slippery, and you would never be able to catch my tail in the same place twice.

"We are still best mates, and time has only tightened the bond between us. Ilir has become a talented sculptor and one of his works is currently displayed in the centre of Municipality K.

When he is 'taking a break', I mean without a job, he roams with his art associates in exhibitions and biennales that take place in different countries.

As for Besian, he emigrated for a better life and decided to come back only two years ago, but things have gone downhill for him, and today he is incarcerated. A harrowing journey indeed."

"I truly feel bitter," murmurs Sherif, " what happened to that poor fellow?"

"It is complicated. A collar-and-tie blockhead's affair which ended in a family tragedy."

"Send my caring thoughts to him and may the porridge in Pompey go light on his belly." says Sherif, shaking his huge, bearish head.

"I will, but by the way, how did things turn out for yourself? Why did you suddenly disappear from the workshop and the neighbourhood?" I ask him.

"My story is quite tangled, and a bit long to narrate. Therefore, you have to bear with me if you would like to hear a piece of it."

"Never mind, I am off from work today. I am all ears." I say to him.

In the meantime, the bar where we are seems to shake to the rafters, and as somebody enters or exits the place and the door opens, plumes of cigarette smoke and din of noises blow out, unloading on the street like small snow avalanches.

"It was the beginning of December," Sherif begins to limn his account, "when one day in the afternoon, two men in knee-length overcoats went up and down the neighbourhood, engaging various people and random passers-by.

After visiting all the shops in the area, they finally stopped at my workplace. One of them had slightly protruding jaws, big brown eyes, and whizzed some goofy tune out with each breath he took and every word he spoke, while the other's posture was as stiff as a ramrod with curly hair and an aquiline face.

'Comrade Sherif?' the frizzy-haired guy addressed me.

'Yes, that is I.' I replied, 'How can I be of any service to you gentlemen?'

'You should come with us.' they replied in one voice.

At that time, it was a common occurrence that when one of the few automobiles in circulation owned by the state had a flat tyre and was stuck on the road, I'd grab my tools and the essential materials with me and go to repair it.

'Yep, in a second, here I come.' I told them, ' I'll just get my stuff and I'll be there.'

'Nope, there is no need to.' both of them answered me at the same time again, 'Shut the workshop and come with us.' the guy with a whistling sound in his voice spoke firmly.

'On the spot.' I answered

I locked up the shop and once they clasped me between them, off we went side by side. We were like one and the same body. We even took the steps in synchrony with each other, as if at one moment performing a military parade, and at another like we were spinning a folk dance…"

At these final words, Sherif is bewildered for a few seconds and starts to whisper through his teeth "At that time, when everything was owned by the state, so much so that you couldn't call your soul your own, it wasn't an oddity for some faceless bureaucrat with chic boots and an iron fist in a velvet glove to fetch you, clip your wings and pack you wherever he fancied. Then the saying went 'wherever the … needs it'. And so the 'new men', though it wasn't anything like that at all, at most it can be said that it was 'a new figurine', who wasn't led by the superstitions or primitive customs, but from a small group of people with eternal power, which had given themselves the right to create laws, and for others to follow them blindly, at all events this man remained an alienated being without hope of being freed from the threads of this suicidal mechanism. My craft has taught me through the years that every bicycle wheel, no matter how perfect it may be, sooner or later will need dishing.

Anyway, as I was walking side by side with those two men that showed up at my workshop without giving any beforehand notice, and after I evaluated in my consciousness with a qualm of terror all of my dodgy actions in the last two decades and it didn't ring a bell to me that I had diverted from the Party's guideline, I asked my two fellow travellers 'Companions, where are we off to?'

'We are under our superior's order to escort you to the headquarters, where they will explain everything to you in detail.' answered the hook-nose fellow, 'We have no other information. We simply execute the warrant.'

There was no way I didn't understand that something fishy was going on, but losing my wits wasn't a choice for me in those conditions. Therefore, I had to kiss the rod, and in keeping my composure, I walked side by side with the two contracted-faced undercover agents. Shortly after, we arrived at the entrance of a retractable roof cinema, which was shut down since it was winter, and there was not a soul to be seen around the place. The main wooden door, which incorporated small squares of frosted glass, was padlocked with thick links shackles. At the end of the wall was a crimson sheet metal hatch that had to be the employee's entrance. We knocked, and somebody stared from the peephole inside and opened the door. We walked through a narrow passage to the main square, where the films are shown during summer. A crowd of people gathered there was bursting with a whoop and a holler, giving piggybacks in a free-for-all environment. What struck me was that everybody had turned their backs to the giant outdoor screen fabric and were positioned facing the main building. The surrounding walls were painted a dull yellow, and green-striped benches ran sideways along the two-storey structure. On the first floor, the windows were shuttered from the inside with wooden casements, painted green too, while on the second floor, in the middle of the façade of the building, the projection film port drew everybody's attention.

A man stood in one of the upstairs windows, his arm raised. At times he appeared to be saluting the crowd and at another time as if he was giving directions to people inside the room. I and my two companions threaded our way through this human throng skirting the wall, and we headed towards the building. As we got in, I came across an excruciating emptiness, and because of the humidity inside, water bubbles formed on my eyebrows and eyelashes, and I started to toil with my respiration.

The cheers from outside were soon drowned out by the clickety-clack of an immense number of typewriters from rooms on both sides of the corridor, pecking the rubber platen inexhaustibly. A multitude of people, they too wearing overcoats, were buzzing around with paperwork on their hands.

We went up to the first floor, and the two escorts handed me over at an office, where the man that I had seen on my way in was still motioning to the crowd from within, and then the two fellows accompanying me left. The waving man was trying to say something, but the words he could utter were muffled and mumbled. It was impossible to make any sense out of it, except that he was blabbering while slurring as if he had marbles in his mouth. Up close, I could see his face was pockmarked and veined with bulging red capillaries. Beside him stood a sculpture that was moulded to reflect a man with his hand raised, to which he was tied inseparably with transparent glass pipes and was giving his best effort to imitate.

Across the room, beside him, there was a table with twelve other people standing there, seated in a row, who were sketching on papers, glancing at that human shadow from time to time as he waved his hand, with him ever more so resembling an embalmed corpse. As they finished their sketches, every one of them folded the papers afterwards and slipped them through a postal box placed beside the door. One of them, a paunchy, chubby-necked fellow, almost bald-headed apart from a few hairs on the back of his head that he had grown and tangled to form a single lock that looked like a rat's tail, asked me to sit in the chair that was standing in front of the desk.

After he had a deep breath, he grumbled and, while rubbing his forehead, told me 'Sherif, Sherif, Sherif! Much tribulation you bear. You have to confess in order to break free. Do you know what I mean? A heavy burden you are carrying on your shoulders.'

'I always hand over all the excess materials and leftovers to the head office at the end of each month. Those are all registered on the inventory. My conscience would never have been at ease, even if a single nail were to be missing.' the words poured at once out of my mouth.

'Shut your word hole; I'm not talking about darts nor about razor blades. You cannot ambush someone with pins and needles, but about something much graver and more serious. Through your action or inaction, and we have kept a weather eye on you for a long time, you have been nurturing wrong ideas among the citizens. It is better for you to spew your guts out, for if we unfastened the sack (clenching his fist and swinging it at me menacingly), you'll be left a double vent sack.' he keeps snapping at me.

'I lead a regular life without excesses. Very rarely do I go out and meet a friend at the factory city's council. Even then, when we do meet, we talk about the new production norms given to us as guiding principles from the leadership and how best to exceed them.

With my mother, with whom I live, occasionally we have light-hearted debates about which is more beneficial, the loom weaving crafts or those that are created by the latest cloth processing manufacturing. In my opinion, though, I embrace the idea of the high quality of the loom craft, as well as the emotional aspect when you see from start to finish your end product, while the multicolour threads wave, for example, a mat or a dress, still the crafts cannot compete with the benefits that come from mass production in plants and factories, even though the quality does not score as high.'

'Hearken to me!' the paunchy man intimidated me further, 'Not married, affirmative. Not very sociable; you got that under your belt. You teach the kids in the neighbourhood how to stand up against their parents' advice, which makes us doubt that there is more to it. And our reasonable suspicion constitutes a possible risk of action that you may take in the future. And this we do not tolerate by any means.' he concluded his sentence by standing up. He went by the window, looked out into the crowd, and crossed his arms over his chest, pausing thoughtfully for a moment, and then spoke 'See those people down there? They are the film crew members who have been carefully selected from among the folks. Everyone is eager for the film rays that we unleash from here to every home via the TV screens. And we are very eager for their blind obedience and their unwavering loyalty. Of course, the flares can't shine far without burning someone. Since time immemorial, God has endowed us with a leader, whose body, or the better part of him, we have preserved in this sculpture from generation to generation. And every ruler in all epochs tries to resemble him, like our current leader.

While they from below see the radiant flares that we emit from here, from above, we observe the gathering clouds threatening their souls, wherefrom our current leader draws forth his inspiration and tries to articulate to us by means of gestures. And our task is to outline every flick of his, every shift of his posture, and alter it into guidelines and instructions for the general public. And whoever retaliates even slightly against this regime that we have imposed necessarily seeks to cause sedition. And for this reason, under the agitprop article and the forming of a gang to overthrow the people's government, charges which are punished without mercy and with an iron fist, it is good for you to speak up and show your accomplices before it is too late.' he concluded by clenching his right hand and squeezing it tightly, so much so that his whole body began to quake.

'Dear comrade…'

'Head-director,' he filled in.

'… I am neither the first nor the last person on this planet to be single. I cannot be blamed for being unlucky in love, so at least respect me in my misfortune. Secondly, for the accusation that I am less sociable, it is not at all true that I turn my back on society but on the contrary, this happens because I am careful in the selections I make. When I make a friend, my desire is to have an everlasting relationship. As for the children, it pains me to see them with tear marks on their faces after their parents have reprimanded them, not to mention the fact that many of them are hit. Isn't this a tragedy!?

Is it not the first ruler himself, whom every leader worships and strives to emulate, who said that the word should fill the hearts of men and convince them, who by his example taught us that our souls could not be won at gunpoint?'

'Yes, as true as the fact that he was the first to put his chest against the muzzle of the guns. How many of you can do the same?' he kept ranting and raving at me even more fiercely than before 'Guard, take this class decadent and kick him out of my sight.

The two escorts entered and grabbed me by the arm, same as before, but this time their pincer-like hands exerted an even greater force as if to convey without words, from the intonation of the chief director's voice, the sentence taken, and they carted me off to one of the rooms on the ground floor.

There was very little furniture inside it. A steel nightstand, a few chairs, and a desk made of unpolished beech wood, the indent and skelf of which I carried for a very long time on my body and face, after interrogational torture procedures.

A metal-rimmed lamp dangled from the ceiling, casting a dim yellow light across the room. A little further on the only desk standing there, there was a typewriter, behind it, a dwarfish figure would sometimes appear to the left and sometimes to the right, and then slowly poking his head above it, would watch with inquisitive eyes every muscle I twitched.

With every stroke of that typewriter, my flesh was cut into one hundred pieces, my bones crumbled and my joints split open, and blood mixed with saliva and other bodily secretions spewed out, so much so that even I did not believe that my soul had such a secret, underground lake, so deep.

The afternoons came and went with plumes of tobacco and the jeers of the investigating agents, who wandered around the room in an elliptical motion, the same as the faint-light swinging lamp, and me, who stammered at every accusation they slandered with the single phrase 'Innocent'.

Then, when they had their fill and pulled what they were seeking out of you, they would bang their own drum to each other about how they had terror-stricken X-person and had coerced such and such other poor soul to confess and sign a fabricated charge. For if they couldn't petrify you to your marrow, they'd lose their grip entirely and very easily jump down your throat and be diligent in their craft until dawn.

In the meantime, I languished in my cell night after night with the others. And while we were trying to hold ourselves together from the many inflicted wounds and psychological terror we experienced, we fell asleep leaning on each other crosswise, as the cries and pleas that most of us let out in our dreams, or unconsciously as we fainted dead away, resonated.

I have seen so many people being taken completely withered away from that cruel sarcophagus. Days, weeks and months passed with me cooped up until suddenly, the cell door opened, and I was called forth. From there, I was put into exile together with my mother, who at that time was in her eighties. Maybe if I had not kept a stiff upper lip and had accepted their false accusation, my fate would be unknown. And long after that, while in exile, the only word I could utter for months as my mouth trembled was the word 'Innocent'."

As Sherif was narrating this last part, he had turned into a shadow of himself. Pale around the gills and with his chin twitching like a perch, he spoke in a dropping voice, almost fading away.

Although there was a lot of chattering in the bar, I was hanging on to his every word, so much so that I could absorb the meaning of every single word, even though I could not hear a sound coming out of his mouth. It was enough for me to snatch the words from his lips to be well away.

"It was an alpine village," Sherif continues to narrate "where I suffered the years of exile. It is located on a plateau between two mountains and at its piedmont, on its southern side, stretched a lake, which also marked the border with other villages. While to the north of it, at that time, was located a police station, from which point onward oscillates the succession of mountain ranges with bare slopes and steep cliffs. All in all, it is a fistful of land with a punishing climate and limited hours of sunshine. About three to four hours in winter and a pinch more in summer. However, its beauty was well-adjusted and balanced by the lake that was filled in the spring with white lilies, which, according to the legends, happens because a lonely naiad combs her hair on its shore.

There were many other souls like ourselves in that place. We lived in very harsh conditions, in wooden shacks built from scratch by ourselves, and we did menial labour the whole time we spent there. We managed to eat somehow and kept our spirits alive with bites of bread.

Later, I found out that the investigator who interrogated me was from this region, two villages away, which surprised me immensely. Many times, I wondered what crimes these villagers living in that area had possibly committed.

The first few years were also the most difficult, as we had to adapt to the harsh conditions we encountered there, but little by little, I learned to love that place with all my heart. There was something majestic about it, which fascinated me and made me converse without articulating a sound with the shadows of the trees, the crystal waters of the wellspring, the moon during the long fair nights, and everything around seemed to want to communicate to me something of itself.

And when the political system collapsed, and we were able to walk free wherever we chose, I decided to live on a similar plateau, not far from where we had been banished for so many years, but with a more suitable climate, where I still live to this very day. It was impossible for me to depart from that mud and scum. Those days kept raking over the ashes when we lived with just enough to keep body and soul together, as the burning tears dripped into the lake of sorrow in the wrinkled and clenched hands of my mother.

Her caress that shook off the dust and rejuvenated the stiffened muscles caused by malnutrition and excruciating fatigue while we were working our souls' case out appears in my dreams every night.

She gave me her last kiss before she left this world with the same love and hopes as the first time she held me in her arms when I was born. Her generous heart helped any fellow convict as if he were her own son. Her unconquerable spirit that did not bow to any hardship and enormity aimed towards our family, as well as her lullabies that ripped the dark mask of the night when I woke up sweating from nightmares and bad dreams, are the memories that still hold me bound to this blessed land.

Her voice still reverberates in those caves and mountain slopes, especially when the wind blows wild."

As soon as he utters that final sentence, Sherif fell into silence for a while, and a warm tear traces its way down his cheek. In the bar, the scattered noises here and there fade, and the people pause from what they are saying for a few moments, staring at the door as it suddenly cracks open from a gust of wind barging in from outside.

Then, one of the staff members makes their way over and pulls it shut again, and with that, my conversation with Sherif slips into shooting the breeze and sipping a little snakebite medicine, while digesting a few distant memories. The time elapses lavishly.

He goes on to tell me how he spent his time doing a little bit of livestock rearing and farming. He had also been able to build a small reservoir near a stream that flows down from the top of the mountains and has modified it to breed fish. He keeps what he needs for daily use, and he goes out and sells the rest in the mart down the town. He seems quite content with the life he is leading, and also he feels that there is nothing left to bind him to the city life anymore.

We promise each other that we will meet again at the first opportunity, and after exchanging addresses and phone numbers, we part with great fondness. Out on the street, the townsfolk and traffic have thinned out, and every now and then, you could see a dog elegantly throwing its paws at the nearest dustbin.

The tops of buildings still reflect the last, washed-out rays of the sun as the night crawls up the city like a heavy, tenebrous cloak, slowly and meticulously devouring entire districts.

The billboards above the shopfronts and along the side of the roads, with the variety of bright lights and colours, beckoned me for a stroll around the many bars in the city centre before I went home, where I drifted off to sleep in my room over the childhood photo album.

* * *

The next day, the morning bursts forth by lightning, shimmering and flickering the chimneys and antennas on the terraces of the buildings. Apparently, the weather, with the stubbornness characteristic of the spring season, seeks to swap the record whenever it feels like satisfying its caprices. A wetness, as it moistens my cheek, wakes me up, and a salty taste lingers on my tongue as it drips over my lips. I open my eyes slightly, and I see that looking at me with tearful eyes is Ikun, one of the residents with whom I share the house where I live. We have been the longest-staying tenants here ever since we were students. The lodgers who live in the other rooms come and go frequently. Sometimes, even we are surprised when a new resident, freshly arrived, breezes into the kitchen making free with food and drinks from the refrigerator before even introducing themselves.

"Why are you so sad, Ikun? What happened?" I ask her, "Are you upset again with your supervisor at work because he puts all the burdens on you, as well as the failures, while he takes the credit for himself? Or did your fiancé disturb you with an undue word or two after a glass too many?"

"Neither one nor the other." she answers, wiping her tears, "I've taught myself not to fall prey to petty trifles, and in the end, a clear conscience does not have to invent dishonest excuses. Higher in command than my supervisor is someone else in the hierarchy, and no matter how hard one tries, the veil may hide the face but it cannot hide the bride. This can never happen. The prejudices that bother me while practising the profession that I care for so deeply, instead of discouraging me, trigger me to work harder. As for my fiancé, whenever he drinks, which he does only on special occasions, he would never get into a drunken brawl, as he is a lamb of God and not a Hogan's goat."

She walks to the window and, with great finesse, extends her spindly left hand, girded with bracelets, braids and trinkets that jingle, as if to warn of the presence of some drifting yearning for sirocco and begins to draw silhouettes and lines gliding the pulp of her index finger over the glass.

"Do you not understand? You're the one who has annoyed me." she says while moving her hand up and down, "Lately, we haven't seen each other even for the morning's tea and sympathy. Yesterday, you were off from work, but you didn't show up all day. Don't make me feel a draft in this house. We have not hidden anything from each other since we first met."

"I hate it when you blame me for all the calamities on this planet." I reply, smiling, "However, your warning voice is never harmful, no matter how sharp it sounds. And how on earth can it even pass through your mind that I'm avoiding you to make you feel bad? If you weren't going to be any longer in this house, not only would I not stay a moment longer either, but the streets and alleys of this city would be longing to hear the sound of my footsteps as I walk on them. How many times have we talked about the night shift being heavy and rough, even if you don't have a great deal of work to do? It's enough that you have to stay on call all the time. During which the slightest inconvenience alarms you and makes you edgy. And when you wake up in the morning, I've just gone to bed. Though I'm asleep I sense you as in a dream, talking around the house. Yet when I wake up, everything you said is cloudy and blurred, your being is closer to me than anything else in this endless ocean of things we call our world. Afterwards, every day when I wake up, I sniff a whiff of your perfume that has wafted into the hallway, and it feels like we've just been together.

Yesterday I ran into a charming old man whom I have known since I was a child. Unfortunately, he was incarcerated and then exiled for a long time. His story was a true horror, where the saga of state crimes and atrocities was hidden behind collegial decisions. This is also the reason why we did not have a chance to get together yesterday to spill the tea, as we are in the habit of doing so during my days off from work. And when I got home last night, there was no light coming from your room, so I didn't want to disturb you. But no worries, I'll pop the kettle on and make a builder's tea, which will put a smile back on our faces as compensation." I tell her and get ready to get out of bed.

"You keep hiding something from me T." Ikun still insists, "Your eyes are more humble than usual, your body is more bent, and without you noticing, although you try to cover all this behind a flattering smile, you always end the sentences with a groan.

No matter how well you act, you cannot mask it out. You simply cannot sugar-coat the pill to me. Don't tell me that cunning slut has shown up again."

"Who are you talking about?" I ask her.

"It's her." she mumbles to herself.

"Please, that person you have in mind, not only have I not seen her in ages, but even if I met her, she would not make any impression on me whatsoever. That old flame has burned out a long time ago. Time has wiped her name away like waves washing over letters written on the shore with a stick."

"Then tell me why every sign that vibrates on your face speaks of her? I know that sometimes I am quick to make wrong inferences. I really wish that this were the case, too, because I can't bear to see you go through such a period of disappointment again, as happened a few years ago when the shadow drew you to haunted corners."

"And I don't know if I would be the person I am today without you. But since then, many things have changed. Not in the sense that I closed myself off and lost my trust in people. On the contrary, it would not make sense to shut that door, but nowadays, I am the first to ambuscade myself, and so my heart is open to everything. You're right, though, when you say that I may have seemed worried to you, but the cause of that is the imprisonment of Besian, my childhood friend. With all the troubles and worries he had to face recently, what happened to him a few days ago really caved in hard on him."

"How foolish that I am sometimes. It didn't occur to me at all, knowing how close you two are. It's very shocking what happened, and I hope his soul finds redemption in one way or another. Do not move from the bed. I'll go brew some fresh tea, and prepare breakfast."

"All righty then, I'm coming, and we'll prepare it together." I say to her and then I rise up on my elbows, leaning on the back of the bed, "I can't lie down any longer.

Go ahead so I can get dressed, and I'll be there right away."

Meanwhile, Ikun leaves the room, and I get ready to reach for the clothes on the stool, but I see they are no longer where I had put them last night. I look around, but I don't see them anywhere. I go to the wardrobe to check in there, but it is empty. I open the drawers of the nightstands one after the other. Those were empty, too. In the room, everything was in its place, except for the clothes and the liners. Those had disappeared into nothing. Behar is the first person coming to my mind, a glow worm that three weeks ago, Ikun and I found sloshed to the gills under a bush on the side of the road in the early hours of the morning, not far from a kebab shop. The temperatures were below zero, and we thought that if we left him to his fate, he would probably freeze to the point of being a candidate for a pair of wings, so we carried him home with us. Although advanced in age, he has an iron-out-wrinkled face, and when he has fallen asleep, he looks all wool and a yard wide. As for his family, when we asked him about them, he didn't answer us but just snorted like a raging bull with bloodshot eyes, looking around as if scorching hot vapours were coming out of the floor and walls to suffocate him. It was obvious that, whatever the case, it was a sad story, so we didn't push the discussion in that direction any further.

The next day, when he woke up, we found out that he had been living rough since he could remember, and the only relatives, friends and spouse he had was his booze. He kept a white Panama hat on his head and wore a military green jacket. He had icy blue eyes, and his body was skinny and not very tall. Every time he pondered before saying something, he would rub his upper lip with his front teeth, and then he would fire as a wind-up toy, swirling his small palms in the air. He has an exquisite sense of humour, and we grew fond of each other almost instantly. By pure chance, two of the rooms in the house where we lived were unoccupied and ready to rent, so we arranged for him to live in one of those, and Ikun and I would cover his expenses.

"Ikun, I can't find my clothes," I call her from the halfway open door "someone entered my room and cleared everything away. Ask Behar if he knows anything about it."

"What? How is that possible?! Ah T., I forgot to tell you that Behar had an accident yesterday evening while crossing the road in the city centre. His eyesight deteriorated as a result of inebriation, and because of the blurry vision, he did not notice a puddle of water right in front of him. He dived in with both feet and slid wide over it. His pelvic wall collapsed and he broke his shinbone, so he had to have a surgical intervention, and the doctors had to fit a metal plate in his leg. He is now resting in intensive care, and the medical personnel will keep an eye on him until he gets better. They are already taking care of him at Hospital No. 3. Anyway, I have a few spare garments from my fiancé lying around that should fit you. I'm going to get them right away."

The clothes were a little snug across the shoulders and thighs, but somehow, I managed to squeeze into the trousers and shirt that she brought me.

Ikun cooks a finger-licking good breakfast. Ham, sausage, fried eggs, milk and honey. After we chew and savour every bite of the food in front of us, she asks me if I have time to go with her to visit Behar in the hospital. I want to, but at this time, I feel so knackered. The night before, even though I never woke up, I did not have a restful sleep at all. It was as if I were drifting between dreams, and any moment as I was about to be awakened, a thin, sleepy string, extending beyond the unconscious, would pull me back into fragmentary dreams, one after the other to infinity. A vicious circle that hung over me until Ikun cut its thread in the morning. So, even though I am eager to see Behar, I pass on the offer on this occasion and tell her to send greetings on my behalf and to wish him a speedy recovery.

She twists the muffler around her thin, milk-coloured neck, puts the red hood on her head, and, as she goes out, she tells me that a missive is delivered for me.

Besian's name is written on the corner of the white envelope. Unable to meet him in person, as detainees are only allowed to be visited by close family members and lawyers, the only way to communicate with each other is through mail. And this is the first letter he has sent me from detention.

I remember when we were in the second year of high school, and he had to make his way out into the world as an immigrant. It was a time when people poured out across borders, like at the Berlin Wall when it crumbled. He left behind his mother, father and younger brother. Before he left the house, in the last moments, resting his head on his mother's lap, his almond-shaped eyes reddened, and two drops of tears slipped down his cheeks. And then he went away, with his hair all messed up, wearing corduroy the round the houses, a tartan dock jacket, and clodhoppers that were too loose, as those were a size or two bigger than his feet.

The years rolled by one after the other, and finally, two springs ago, he returned back home. As soon as he arrived, he got engaged to a girl who had been a neighbour in the apartment where his grandmother and grandfather lived, in a coastal town, whom he visited during the summer, spending most of his holidays there. Ever since, while playing with his friends, he had accidentally walked over a doll's house she had built in the hall of the building, and after he helped her to reassemble it, they had never been separated. You could say they were in love at first sight since they were kids, if such a thing is possible.

Besian didn't talk about the life he spent in emigration. And each time others asked him about it, he gave a general description without picturing many details and always wrapped up his argument with the sentence "It was no Elysian Fields." After some time, during a routine police check on the street, some seeds of a plant that sweetly plucks the dreams of youth were found in his pocket, and that was enough to arrest and accuse him in court as a prominent trafficker and criminal. This happens at a time when this plant is the most cultivated in the gardens of any authority. However, since he had not been convicted before, the court sentenced him to a conditional release with a probation period of one year. This made him withdraw into himself, and in his conversations with others, he became irritated over the smallest and most insignificant things. He had lost his job, as he was now considered a person who presented high social risk, while the family income had been sucked dry by ambulance chasers, money mules, prosecutors and judges. One day, in an argument with his father, he lost his temper and gave him a shove, and while sliding back, he lost his footing and fell down, hitting the back of his head hard on the floor. Unfortunately, there was nothing that could be done, and his father left this world instantly as he touched the ground. And that, sadly, is the story of my mate, whose soul languishes in the cell.

I sit on the sofa, open the envelope and start reading "What's going on T.? I didn't open the letter you sent me a few days ago right away. I've lost track of time, and every day feels just like the day before. Most of the time here, I lay down and rivet my eyes on the particles of light that filter through the palm-wide chink in the wall, and I must have put on a few pounds. Besides myself, there are three other inmates with me in a room of ten square meters, including the toilet, and we are locked up almost all day, except for one hour, when we have the right to go out in the yard airing.

The fellow convict who shares the twin bed above me is called Erald, a priggish fellow who tries to shoe everybody's mule. He has small eyes and short eyelashes, with fine jaws and a hatchet face. He is a recidivist, and in the punishment that will be announced by the court this time for the theft of a vehicle mirror, he risks being sentenced to at least two years in prison. When, in the ongoing conversation, someone from the opposite cell expressed surprise that he was married because he looked far too young, I was impressed by his reply when he said, 'My kid has become as big as a *ccc*onvict.' pronouncing the letter 'c' hard and following his slang with a sly laugh.

Buiar is bunked up after me, with George utilizing the top bunk. Buiar has a solid body with broad shoulders and a huge, square head. He is a guy who listens to his better angels, and before he expresses himself, he ponders well what he is about to say. On the back of his left hand are tattooed four dots in the shape of a square and a dot in the middle, representing the cell's four walls with him in the middle. He was previously convicted of aggravated robbery, and now he is charged with resisting law enforcement during a routine control at a checkpoint.

George, a short, dark-skinned lad with rough hair that sticks up like a brush, is smiling constantly, although sometimes when he gets really jumpy, it's better to stay out of his way. He is otherwise known as the 'Gat', and he was arrested for firearm and weapon offences.

Yesterday, we were cobbling together a makeshift boiler to heat water, since here in detention, the taps do not have any hot water running inside the cell, and we are only allowed to go to the shower room twice a week. After stripping a triple socket with a switch and undressing both wire tips corresponding to lines one and two, respectively, metal plates were placed on each end. And you cannot imagine the trouble we went through to find those two metal plates, since sharp metal objects are strictly prohibited in here. Finally, I winged it and cut off the end of the broom's stick, which consists of a light aluminium tube, elastic enough not to be considered dangerous for keeping in the custody areas. However, its composition allows the conduction of an electric current well enough. We also put a rubber stopper between the two plates in order not to make a short circuit and fry our brains out. And while we were getting all this done by creating a live wire, I cherished the childhood memories of how we used to put together swords, crowbars, and all kinds of self-made toys. I am not sure if you remember that one time when we ran across an antique radio thrown away behind the main building, and we all rushing in to hack it apart, kicking it or striking it with whatever we had in our hands. At that moment, Ilir told us to hold our horses and proposed that it would be better if we disassembled it to have a look at how that byzantine machine worked from the inside. Then, he leapt at the task with such attentiveness, which has always been his speciality. Taking a screwdriver from his pocket, he began hacking away at the screws one by one. And the rest of us, observing him, racing to make haste slowly in order to help him out, like nurses in an operating room. Oratory has never been one of his hidden talents, but stones and wood, of whatever kind, after carving them masterfully with chisels and fingers, Ilir makes those worth a thousand words. Tiny bits of that 'habit' has stuck with me too. As soon as I was done with the water heater, I opened the envelope you had sent me earlier in custody. While reading it, my soul demolished the walls of the cell and wandered somewhere in the streets of our hood and the city. Your smile, voice and movements spanned along with the words on paper making them truly come alive, granting me the gift of a few flashes of freedom. The sweeter those moments tasted, when my mind and soul were as free as the air, the more bitter was the reality afterwards.

Everyone knows that I'm locked up in here for murder, but they don't know that the person whose life I took was my own father. I haven't told them because it's still too hard for me to cope with what has happened.

The chandelier at the top of the house is smashed to pieces, and I bleed hereafter in the dark by the thousands of glass panes that crackle under my feet every step that I take. Will there be light for me at the end of the tunnel? Ah, how mortifying I feel for my mother whose bed I left dry and her son far away. She tries to take care so that I lack nothing, starting from food to clothing, because in here, apart from iron bars, electricity and a scheduled water supply, you have to provide and bring everything else by yourself. I'm locked in the cage, and my mom, a slave of my cruel luck out there. Misfortunes never come singly!

When things get unbearable in the house of many doors, the conversations that bring in a breath of fresh air are the back-of-the-envelope calculations that we make of the possible years we are going to spend in the dungeon. Buiar claims that if he had felt his collar two months later, he would have been able to secure as much income from his profitable shady 'activities' as he needed in order to grease the palm of the judge or the prosecutor with oil of angels. As a result, everyone would be happy with a smile fixed on their faces. 'Dosh,' he says, repeatedly rubbing the thumb with the tip of his index and middle fingers, 'a golden key that can open any door.'

Meanwhile, George has bestowed the *tocher* and he waits for the messenger any day now with a happy announcement. His mother always fetches him homebaked cakes, which, according to local superstitions, means that she has put his affairs straight, and the good news of his release will not take long to be delivered.

While Erald is afraid of the fact that he will receive the highest possible sentence because, firstly, he is a repeated offender; secondly, the crime was ordinary; and, thirdly, he could not afford to cover the court expenses, and as a result, he also had an attorney free of charge, appointed by the law.

As for me, I pinned all my hopes on the act of the expertise to mark the death as accidental, although in itself, the subject does not impress me the slightest since no flow of time can wash my father's blood from my hands.

Every time I discuss this with Buiar, he always advises me to state that I committed the act in self-defence, and he doesn't understand why it didn't occur to me to emphasize this in the first confession I made in front of the police. Then, seeing me not giving an answer in response but just sighing and turning my head to the other side, he further adds, to comfort me, that it is normal to forget crucial details when you are in a state of psychological trauma.

And he spurs me on to mention this to the prosecutor as soon as possible before the investigation is closed and the case is sent for trial.

Eh, dear T., I am convinced even more as each day passes that a group of unscrupulous people, in the name of justice and society, keep us locked inside this Cyclops' cave and, from time to time, watch us through the prison porthole, to see how fat we are getting. On the one hand, they beat their chests in front of society and boast that, as long as they are in charge of affairs, they are out of any danger. On the other hand, they skin us alive and have the underprivilege's guts for garters for the reason that they are not capable of hoodwinking and stealing enough from society to pay them the obligatory tribute. As a result of this dichotomy, people without support and skills in underground money muling are punished harshly, and on many occasions unjustly, to cover up the crimes of those who have support from authority. And if the perpetrators are not punished, it is useless to deal with the effects of a perverted conscience because news spreads fast in a small country like ours, where a punishment unjustly given to one and the undeserved release of another simply adds fuel to the flames, and the fire is a good servant but a bad master.

Here, the hearings are held right after the dead of the night. When the hounds that watch us over at custody fall silent, and their growl is dissipated and completely absorbed by the liquid darkness of the sky, right when the moon and the stars shine ever more brightly, a creature that looks like a kangaroo visits us at the porthole. But instead of front legs, it has two powerful forceps and a television-shaped second head extension that juts out from its tummy pouch, to whom it speaks, exchanging remarks explaining the reasons why each of us should be locked in here, waiting in the end for the verdict made by her, which seals the deal.

On his back, you can still make out the eyelet, where the reins used to be fastened, since, according to the legends that circulate in here, this creature is descended from the horses that were once wild and free, then tamed to serve in the entourage of the tribal coachman. And when the charioteers got down with their feet on the ground, throwing away the reins because some just got tired of it and others were overthrown because everyone already had their own way to follow, they metamorphosed into what they are today. For all those who know this transformed being and have had anything to do with him, Ervin Karanjella is nothing but a money grabber, who feeds on random nonsense and scraps of miserable people. In short, he is a bogus being and a systemised gulper. After he clings with his two forceps to the iron bars at the door of our cell supported on his tail and knocks on it cheerfully with his rear legs, he begins to speak, addressing his extension 'Your Honor! I don't know if these walls are made of honey, and they think that it may be a hive, that these insects keep swarming back, or what?... Ah, just look what we have in here, there's a fresh meat arrival.' addressing George, 'Accused of possession of a firearm without a permit. Well, namby-pamby, what bothers you that makes you feel insecure and forces you to carry a gun? Don't you like our toil and sweat in every corner of the country, preserving human integrity and repelling evil from the doorsteps of your homes?!'

'Your Honor!' George addresses the television shape extension, "I see that in the body of the prosecutor shines new fur, but his sweat has the same stench as his predecessors, all fur coat and no knickers. He belongs to a race carefully chosen to guard our vineyards, though the scarecrows themselves used to do a bang-up job, far better than he ever could.'

'We will see how much your skin is worth.' says Ervin Karanjella, grinding his teeth, 'I request that the defendant be held in custody.'

The judge affirms, shaking her head and says 'If you want to get your beauty sleep, though, you need to fork out the dough.'

'Resisting law enforcement, previously convicted of robbery.' Ervin reads the charge facing Buiar, 'Well, master of disaster, all that anger you have inside, why don't you vent it on the sports clubs, which the society we serve so humbly has built for you? Or the savages, but the shackles adorn them?'

'Your Honor! What the prosecutor sees as anger is love that I inherited from my father. I'm just trying to give back *the change* to the society in which he was toughened.'

'We will see *the change* interpreted into prison time.' says the prosecutor mockingly, "I request that the defendant be held in custody.'

The judge affirms, shaking her head and says 'If a bakery's bun fight for you is too much, how is going against the city hall come out all right?!'

'Accused of the theft of a vehicle's mirror, previously convicted of pickpocketing.' the accusation is addressed to Erald, 'Well, leech, why don't you cling to the financial aid the social institutions have calculated so carefully for people in need? Is it not enough for you to see yourself in front of the mirror of our social care, which we have built so meticulously for this occasion?'

'Your Honor! Your relief is alms that slip through my sieve-like conscience, and the mirror you have provided burdens me with ugly goblins; therefore, I look for another one for myself to gild the lily.'

'Ehhh! When the benefit lizard, lower than a snake's belly, strives to become the ball's belle. I request that the defendant be held in custody.'

The judge affirms, shaking her head and pronounces 'Bent as a nine bob note craven, make the dance as for seven!'

'Giving a belt that resulted in a death blow. Previously convicted for the possession of powerful seeds.' finally address me, 'Well, cheeky, good for nothing, don't you like how we wield power to judge what is right and what is wrong? Do you think that people educated not in the finest universities of the world can exercise it more responsibly?'

'Your Honor! If cutting one's wisdom teeth for power required just one university course, I would have gone through fire and water to acquire it, but I fear it is the moment when the impulse is in balance with reason that puts the cap on everything. ('Ahhh, if only I hadn't lost my mind, or my father his balance!' I thought to myself.)

'Blimey! Detention has been enriched with thinkers. You will have plenty of time at your disposal, sir, to crack the nut's secrets of the world.

I request that the defendant be held in custody.'

The judge affirms, shaking her head and saying 'You need a taller lawyer to not rot in the dungeon any longer.'

After reaching the conclusions in our cell, they carried on to the next, where they passed the verdict to release a defendant, who was accused of murder, acquitting him because, according to the investigations, he assumed that he had a toy gun in his hand, and therefore the shooting was considered involuntary.

In another compartment a short distance away from where I am locked up, an individual charged with trafficking in significant quantities of Class A narcotics had his prison sentence conveniently commuted to house arrest.

A few days later, it became known that the address of the house where he was supposed to isolate himself did not even exist and that this person was not only any longer under house arrest but had already lost his trail, an outcome that would not have happened without the blessing of those who baked that abhorring wafer of release.

In short, the villainy in here corrodes your insides faster than death, dear T.

I don't want to linger any further lest I sour your thoughts further with the rotten stink that reeks of hypocrisy in here, and I also want to write something to Edlira. Even though I see her once a week and I call her every day, she doesn't stop crying while we speak on the phone. And when I write a note to her, it is as if I somewhat dissipate her woes and ease her heartache.

I end this writing by fondly embracing you, my friend, from the very den of Hades."

As I fold the paper and place it in the desk drawer, taps are heard at the window, growing louder and louder. The hailstorm unfolds furiously, and a relentless wind conducts what in a brace of shakes in the surrounding nature turns into a chaotic commotion, where tree branches swing around and about, window panes slam, and hanged and forgotten garments on clotheslines flap recklessly. Due to the sudden drop in outside temperatures, the inside of the room's window glass is coated with a misty film of condensed steam, where the faint drawings made by Ikun just a little while ago, while sliding her fingers on its surface, begin to emerge.

Irregular lines, spirals and twists transpose me into foggy thoughts. My eyelids are weary, and I feel utterly helpless in the face of the storm of suffering that any of my friends are experiencing through life's entanglement. A really bitter baton, which we have to pass to each other and which, no matter how much you try to sweeten it, has basically remained unchanged, coarse and insoluble.

Drowsy as I am. time flutters dreamily, till I have to get ready and go to work.

I finally come to my senses as I step outside, where the cool evening air, mixed with the coniferous scent of the fir trees on either side of the road, in two shakes pierces my nostrils and sober me up. Broken branches fallen to the ground, drains choked with debris, and a clear, windless and twinkling night are some of the still fresh traces that the storm has left behind.

The city lies in the grip of silence, so complete that I can hear the soles of my shoes crunching on the asphalt as I walk down the street. From the starry sky, a few sparks break loose and ignite the five-story building of the hotel where I work, which is located not far from the centre but still somewhat tucked away, perched on a hill with a wide view over the city. The rear of the hotel is bordered by the great park of ridges and pines of all kinds, which spreads over and densely coats the mountain neck. And on the right side, the stadium of the local football team rises in the shape of a torch.

The entrance hall is majestically elevated by semi-arches balanced atop capitals of the seven to eight-meter-high columns, and the cream-colored crowns it all, giving the sense you've stepped into another world, where evil flukes and nervous strains are but a bad dream of the past. Yet none of this grandeur would have any meaning at all without the gatekeeper waiting for you at the entrance, or as we call him, the "guardian angel".

He has a very particular role because he is the first person to welcome the guests to the hotel. Like the carpet in front of the entrance door that serves to scrape the mud from the sole of the shoe, so he, with his relaxing smile and his readiness to help, welcomes and relieves the guests who arrive at the hotel from a long and strenuous journey. And in general, the hotel's clientele travels here for business from faraway places. So, the "guardian angel" should be jolly and useful, with an original smile and a somewhat spongy skeleton, as he should be accustomed to anyone who comes here to spend the night. And, preferably, he should slip effortlessly into their hearts instantly, but at the same time, not leave an existential trace in their memory. Each porter must resemble their colleague and radiate the hotel's good name as decently as possible.

Not everyone is cut out for this role because all these talents must be in such proportion that, if any of the parts are lacking, or present in excess, it creates a chain reaction and undoes those other good qualities that he may have, ending up with an outcome that is not at all desirable.

For example, a few years ago, when the previous doorman retired, a brilliant, polite and hard-working young man took over the position. But unfortunately, he was more sensitive than was required, and when a customer threw the suitcase into his hands with all the harshness of a tired traveller, he, on the spur of the moment, flung it back to him, and the suitcase came very close to toppling the poor man topsy-turvy. The vacant position was filled by another guy who completely lacks backbone, and became annoying with a feigned humility, offering help to customers now and then even when it wasn't necessary to do so.

For all the reasons that I mentioned, lucky is the hotel manager to whom an employee with the right qualities falls in the lap, because when they fall, it is an everlasting acquirement since porters, compared to other hotel staff, create more special bonds with the environment, both in intensity and in duration and quality, and see it as a second home, from where, if they are well settled, rarely ever leave.

The front office is lined up further inside. It represents the brain of the hotel's operation and serves as a point of contact between the guests, the different departments and the city with its various events. As a result of these qualities, the receptionists are more refined; they maintain a necessary distance to treat the customers with the respect they deserve, and the gap that the position imposes is recovered by the flexibility in services and the best possible solution to the guest's issues.

Then comes the bar staff, restaurant, room service and management of festive events and various conferences. The main features of the entire team working at the hotel, including me, if you can describe it in a few words, are that it provides fast and reliable service to the guests, as well as creating the most welcoming conditions for them to relax and enjoy themselves while being involved in a variety of activities that take place throughout the year. The departments mentioned are the ones that have the most direct human impact on the clientele, as they are closer to them. And, if you are not careful, you might not notice the string that wraps a bag of candy or sweets, placed on the pillow and the double duvet laid warmly, which invites you to wrap yourself in for a sweet and loosy-goosy sleep, as if in the arms of a swan. Or that even the air conditioning is left running in the room just a short time before the guest's arrival, so the room may absorb the appropriate ambient temperature, as well as detailed and stamped receipts when you check out. Thus, it is very easy to overlook and leave the hotel's housekeeping department in the shade, and that of the engineers, as well as the finance department.

Among these last three, the department closest to my heart is that of the engineers, since all the time, with few, if not primitive, tools, they have to devise all kinds of tricks and use the newest innovations to cope with the innumerable faults that arise as a result of frequent power outages, which are covered by a generator working at full capacity.

Standing at the front desk, scrutinizing me from afar, Hotiana, the manager of the second shift, stands waiting for me. A sun-kissed girl with black hair loose over her shoulders and fringe bangs above her brows.

"As always, walking flippantly, fit for royalty on his way to the throne." she remarks, slightly peering her eyes at me, as she continues observing my face, clearly searching for a touch more inspiration for another flourish to add "You guys from the third shift have such a countenance, coming a little... how to say it..., pale and mysterious, but not in the bad sense of the word, but in a rather noble way, actually."

"Well, we who are spoiled by the moon's rays, dreams smile at us by day. A throne without a portfolio is one of them." I reply with a wink.

"To tell you the truth, I prefer the third shift." she mumbles the words in a fading away voice, while bending over, she is trying to get something out of the drawer on the right landside "Your shift hours fall in the still of the night, and you don't have the commitment and intensity of work we experience in fulfilling the whims of each guest. Because at that time, most of the clientele are either asleep or are half dazed on the grip of the grapes. In any case, easily manageable."

"Trust me, it's not as simple as it seems." I answer as I look, sometimes to my left and sometimes to my right, if any of my colleagues on the third shift have showed up, "As you go into the arms of your loved ones and rock them to sleep, we sing to the owls and bats at night."

"Please, just don't stop the song." she says giggling, as she hands me the arrival list of guests. She takes time filling me in on the latest events in the hotel.

"It is a virtue to be extolled, and it doesn't matter to whom you sing, as long as you have the opportunity to let off some steam that you have garnered inside you. Otherwise, you will start to slouch over and become a humpback. There is no peace for the wicked, so the evil will pour forth somewhere." she tells me while laughing and continues filling me in with the latest news in the hotel.

"We don't have any free rooms tonight, and two more arrivals are expected with the flight after midnight. All the other guests are already comfortable in their rooms, so you don't have much to worry about. It is one of those splendid days that radiates nonchalance everywhere. Even the deputy director is buzzing all the time, cordially meeting everyone who happens to be in front of him. He guarantees customers quality service and gives the staff members a pat on the back and a smile followed by a joke, which goes against his nature. Most recently, he said to the bar's personnel 'Squeeze the bottles dry tonight boys and don't let a drop go to waste, coz' we are not an inn without gates!' she keeps on telling me."

"His good mood may be down to the arrival of the new director, whom I haven't met yet." I say to her, "As you describe it, it sounds very sarcastic. Although at the beginning, they all walk around the hotel's surroundings in order to make the best possible impression on the new director. I don't get it, why the hell do they assign a new director almost every two years? Why are they being circulated so often? It seems to me that the head office does not trust us at all. They complain that we are pushing the directors away from the right path, and then everything goes downhill from there."

"Frankly speaking, those at the head office are right! At least on one occasion. Has it skipped your mind when the former director turned the hotel into a party and gambling club and nearly drove it into the ground? Then, one fine day, the law enforcement officers came and almost confiscated the hotel. The director then had falsified some documents, passing the ownership of the hotel to another player, after the latter had won it fair and square in a gambling game." she tells me, grinning.

"Maybe in that case, the finger of responsibility should be pointed more at his second in command, the deputy director." I tell her, sighing and shaking my head as I remember some not very pleasant events from that time, " He had to take care to keep him on track. But when you are not up to the job, short-sightedness may be deemed as foresight. A few days ago, Karl (that's the name of the deputy director) sacked a waiter, for the reason that he did not put a napkin on the tray before serving, while the luxury expenditure and the improper behaviour that stood out from the director at that time, he could not dictate it in time!" I conclude by twisting my lips in displeasure.

The vice-principal, a skinny tiny chap hollow-cheeked with two dimples that sink into it like two dizzying vortices, gnawing away processed tobacco all the time, and what most impresses one while in his company, is the way, after long periods of silence, he sneaks, like a hawk, from one department to another, to grab the next victim among the employees.

"Oh T., please, don't tell me that you are not impressed by what all the vice-principals, or deputies, who are never crowned as prime directors, have in common..." she says without hiding a sign of surprise on her flattering face.

After taking my time for a few seconds to think, I answer "Maybe hatred and sluggishness towards the other and the dissimilar?"

"More or less. More than hatred, what characterizes them is the lack of love or, rather, the barrenness of independent thinking. But while he is unaware of this shortcoming, having courage in his conviction blames his subordinates for everything, in order to make them feel worthless and miserable. Without realizing it, he is a participant in a double game. On one side stands his superior, the director, as a guiding window and cult of worship, exempt from any infringement. And against him stand the others, uncouth and procreators of a thousand and one evils. In this confrontation, he sees himself as the connecting link, entrusted with the honourable task of dipping his hands up to the elbow with the company's 'scum' to clean up and keep his superior unpolluted in this enterprise. This is their 'holy' war. While we are the rascals inspired to the right way only through the symphony of music that is played on our bodies when they are mercilessly whipped. Man is a cruel animal!"

"That's right, though I don't know if the two of us belong to the domesticated animal species or that of the uncivilised man." I answer her teasingly.

"It is even worse than you think T., as we both belong to the category of automatons, inside of which life does not flow," she replies to me as she gets ready to leave "albeit as one of the simplest forms, where the lever points only up or down."

After taking two steps forward, she turns on her heel, leans in close, whispering in my ear "Watch out for the snooper, because last night he came as a bogey to check out and to watch over the night shift." and she disappears into the turns of the personnel corridor before one could blink.

It is amusing that, although a closed circuit of cameras monitors the hotel, Karl likes to track and observe everything with his own eyes furtively, behind the columns, where he is spotted anyway because his huge shoes betray him, no matter how much he strives to hide.

This type of man belongs to the "old school" class, which trusts no one and nothing but their own eyes. So, surveillance by means of cameras or any other device is regarded as an unnecessary and inefficient tool that can be manipulated very easily.

Meanwhile, I take a second look around to notice the third-shift staff, and as always, Ermal, the most enthusiastic and charming porter who has ever worked here, is chatting with the bartender, exchanging gestures and roaring with laughter.

As the receptionist checks out the guest cards, one of the hotel's gorilla-sized security guards stands outside in the courtyard, signalling to the driver to park his car.

For a moment, my gaze crosses that of Ermal, and then I move on to the lost and found compartment. I turn the key in the lock of the heavy beech door, which, as you push it with difficulty, gives the impression that you are opening the wooden gate of a broch. Suitcases, boxes, furniture and numerous items are scattered around the room, among which I was impressed by a closet covered with shiny, reddish-maroon fabric.

I was contemplating it out of curiosity, and before long, we all gathered to discuss the day's business, as we are accustomed to doing just before the start of the shift.

A few moments of impregnated silence surrounded us. And, as if we are in an exhibition of statues, we look from time to time, without speaking, at each other and the things around us until finally, I speak to disperse the deafness that is becoming utterly suffocating "I am aware that the gate to enter here is quite wide, while the exit is narrower than the eye of a needle. This is best shown by the objects that have been here since time immemorial. Many of these objects have turned, why not, into legends and folk tales that spread from ear to ear with intoxicating whispers. Here, for example, this one-string bowed *lahutë*, found inside a pitcher when the foundations of this building were dug, was sealed with wax as tightly as a drum, thanks to which air and moisture have not penetrated to damage it. Now, this instrument refreshes dull minds with sweet sounds and nectar words rolling away and dissipating the fatigue and boredom that accumulates during working hours. Adjacent to it is a sewing machine, which belongs to Mrs. Lenka, the director of an international financial institute, who was located here to support and control the budgets of several government agencies. Although she created multimillion-dollar budgets and set economic targets that had to be met by various institutions, she still preferred to patch her own clothes or socks when they got holes in them. When she finished her service and was ready to leave, she announced that she would be back again to retrieve the sewing machine, but we haven't heard from her ever since.

I'm sure that when she left, she remembered the envious glances exchanged stealthily by the hotel housekeepers as she got in her car, and that, I think, is the reason why she hasn't withdrawn it to this day. And indeed, not a day goes by that some of the housekeepers do not slip some cloth in it, singing out loud and telling their friends that they can sew the finest and most beautiful seam in the whole town with this machine. But above all else, that closet by the wall impressed me the most when I walked in here. Please, Ermal, can you tell me how it ended up here?"

"You're absolutely right, T., the objects here truly are priceless treasures. But more precious still are the stories they carry." Ermal begins to speak, blinking, from where two small brown and round eyes sweep the entire surface of the room as if by hand span, "One night, during the third shift, the complaints from the VIP floor kept coming because of some strange noises that were heard from time to time, which resembled the wail of the folk mourning, culminating in piercing shrieks in the morning. We tried to calm the hosts, assuring them that everything was fine and that there was no emergency they needed to worry about. We went there to understand where the frightening noises were coming from.

At first, we didn't notice even the slightest sound, and everything was as quiet as an August night at the beach down south when groans were suddenly heard and screams echoed throughout the corridor. It was indeed creepy and made my flesh shudder, for one could not distinctly tell whether it was a single voice or several voices slurred together. We were equally unsure if what we were hearing were human screams. Furthermore, the source of that uneasiness was extremely vague and dubious. First, we assumed the air circulating in the vent pipes was causing that screeching noise, so we turned it off. The result was not at all what we expected, as the cries became sharper, and more so, because the ventilation and the whistling produced by the friction of the air currents with the pipes had until then served as dampeners for the strange groans, which had become such a disturbing issue that night. We thought then of the heaters and the steam circulating in its ducts, but the only thing that changed after we turned it off was the surrounding environment, which became freezing cold. Meanwhile, we also switched off all the electrical equipment on that floor, as well as the elevator's power, hoping that after these measures, nothing would hiss or clatter. But in truth, those squeals became even louder and more bloodcurdling than before. As soon as we suspected that we had spotted the source where the sound was emitted, we headed there, but it was not possible to locate it since those cries were like a current; their source was everywhere, and the cause was nowhere. Finally, somewhere around 3.30 in the morning, our hopes were dashed that we would be able to discover the reasons behind those terrifying noises, to spot the 'she-wolf's howl source', as we would later call it. And finally, we had no other option but to relocate all the guests to one floor below. Right after accommodating them, the screams suddenly stopped, and normality was restored. In the morning, just ahead of the shift's swap, while I was inspecting the floor in question for the last time, I noticed that this lordless kist stood at the end of the corridor. It was locked and latched, and no matter how hard I tried to open it, I couldn't budge it even one bit. After asking all the guests from the night before if this closet belonged to them, and after they all denied it, together with the shift manager, we decided to bring it here until further notice."

Ermal concludes narrating about the events, not taking his eyes off the closet.

"Strange how people abandon their belongings as if they were painful burdens of the past." I answer with my eyes sunken to the floor, "What is important is that none of our customers have lost anything. Whoever is interested in this closet, sooner or later, will come back and ask for it. Also, the fact that the 'she-wolf's howl' was dissipated is no less important, and I hope that tonight we will not hear any howling of wolves or singing of cuckoos. During the night shift, I want nothing but silken cries to flow from anyone's lips and cotton troubles to fall on our heads."

"I don't know if Mrs. B. Bekteshi, who arrives today with a guest, falls under that category." interrupts the receptionist.

Mrs. Bekteshi, this woman who had just embraced the early period of senility, had once been an excellent theatre actress, and the gown of play-roles she carries on her shoulder, as varied as brought with blood and thunder, thanks to her innate talent for acting, had not yet lost their former inspiration. But after an unrequited love affair with a fellow artist, she went through turbulent times, and, not without regrets, she decided to finally retire from the scene. After this sad chapter in her life, she moved abroad across the sea, but deep in her soul, she had cast the anchor of her heart in the deep waters of everyday city life. And she could never tear herself permanently away from it.

Now and then, accompanied by some high-class squire, having fished him somewhere in worldly salons abroad, she would appear around the city pompously announcing her next mission.

The first time she returned back home, she founded a non-profit organization for the rights of animals. It didn't take long for this initiative to die out, as no one took it seriously. This was because the common folk, due to a previous state of marked lack of individual liberty and property ownership, abused their clawed-back rights to justify the seizure of public property and the distortion of the truth in favour of their narrow personal interests, let alone protect the rights of animals, which did not occupy any place at all in the scales of rights at those times. Thus, her animal protection organization was perceived by the people more as an opportunity to receive an income as wages and per diems than as a starting point for more rights of any kind. After hitting the road again, she returned a few years ago with the idea of initiating the opening of a university dedicated to art and culture. As an idea, it deserved to be praised, but when the trend of the time was to give flesh and soul to the art of making money, spending time pursuing aesthetic beauty and local customs was seen as worthless and boring.

And so, each time, her creative intentions experienced a death knell before the end of the season. As a result, she always left sad and heartbroken, just like the first time, only to return again with a new acquisition and the impregnation of new hope.

During her stay in the city, she took up residence in the hotel's finest suites and although voyaging in a pair, she always stayed in a room on her own. She kept a certain distance from her traveling companion and mostly communicated with him by other means than words, through facial expressions and gestures, and especially captivated the poor fellow when, while conversing on a topic, all of a sudden, she interrupted him, ignoring what had been said previously to jump on to another subject. Accordingly, her mannerisms intrigued the unfortunate chap even more as the days went by, and although to anyone else, her attitude would be offensive, to the eyes of those who were caught in her web, those acts were the most graceful they had ever seen in a woman. Strange how love and servility make fluff grow out of your eyes! In the first case, it is caused by the blindness of the object you love, while in the second case, it is the punishment caused by that object that terrorizes you if you do not follow it slavishly on a whim.

I have seen many such stout men, buddies of Mrs. Bekteshi, who at the end of their stay at the hotel were metamorphosed into furry puppies that laughed all the time without a cause or were roaming in the corridors groping and crushed by lust, muttering to themselves. Being a woman who must have kissed the Blarney Stone, when she couldn't get her way with her fascinating behaviour, she would swallow you in her trap of power, thanks to the pathological persistence that she unsheathed, not without nervousness. It was easier to escape from the eye of a cyclone than from a conversation that was taking place while she was talking. And she talked up a storm about everything and nothing.

Therefore, her arrival would require each one of us to bend over backwards, as she spends lots of time staying in the hotel, just as much at the bar as at the conference rooms, where she organizes frequent receptions and speaks in favour of various raised causes.

"Hey guys, do you think this coat suits me?" The security man draws our attention. He has already thrown a cape on his shoulders, which he had found somewhere in the room. He has placed a round hat on his head, too, with a shelter about two fingers of length, and is looking at himself in front of a mirror, taking the most ridiculous poses.

"You have always had a secret service agent's gene in you," Ermal tells him laughing, blending it with a touch of irony " but you are so secretive that the Secret Service has not yet picked you up on their radar to hire you, that's why you're still working here with us as a security guard."

"Would someone kindly explain to this pumpkin how those chicks who came tonight with the excursion organized by 'Telos Tour' were glaring at me. Haven't you noticed in the movies that it is only at secret agents that chicks gaze, with such a seductive look, as they did stare with goo-goo eyes at me?!" the security officer addresses the receptionist.

"Ermal, please don't harass the bouncer. He is the best lad here among us." the receptionist intervenes with a smile, "Just yesterday, this behemoth standing here snatched a woman out of the jaws of death by performing the kiss of life on her."

"Even today, my teeth are still numb." complains the security guard with a sour face, "Eh, her lips were freezing cold."

"With all the huge lungs you have, it's a good thing you didn't split her open or cause a thrombosis in her brain." says Ermal, roaring with mirth.

"Okay, lads, the meeting ends here. As always, you were such a good audience to converse with. And now let's get back to work so that this night will pass as smoothly as possible and without problems." I say to my colleagues on the third shift and walk forward to the secret staff hatchway to get out, " I will be at the office because I have to put together some reports. If you need anything, let me know!"

I walk out of the room and leave the three of them together, making gestures and fooling around with each other in front of the mirror.

Like most hotel back offices, ours is not far from the reception, connected by elongated corridors, wide enough for a person to pass freely through them, like a mole in his tunnel. If two people happen to be in the same corridor, then both would brush their shoulders against the wall, barely managing to pass through. The only one that stands out is the main corridor that leads to the director's office, which ends in a square, where statues of half-naked figures are placed on top of several round marble columns, with a cape thrown over their arms that seem to point in some direction, or as if they are issuing any instructions.

While walking towards the office, I bumped into someone whom I hadn't noticed, as I was keeping my head low.

"'Corto de Luces'[1] where do you go like that without watching your step?" he speaks through his teeth, and who else but Karl, the deputy director, who is originally from Argentina. Now and then, he blurts out a phrase in Spanish, whenever he is startled or fit to burst with anger.

" 'Porquería Matador!'[2]" I answer with an expression that I have picked up from many conversations with Spanish-speaking hosts in the hotel. "You know that these corridors have turned into personal tranches for me, especially these hours when my brain's caught in a sort of moonflow; I don't know if you catch my drift. It is an occupational disease."

"Of course, of course. You gem of the night shine brighter in the moonlight. I know you well. Before I held this position, I used to be one of you."

"Well, this is the best I can do. Not every ox is made to pull every cart. But you, too, have yet to free yourself of the

---

[1] Not the brightest candle in the chandelier

[2] Matador of scumbags

knacks of your former post." I answer, "As for example, insomnia."

"This is why our kind has been selected to be in charge of affairs, since, from the same phenomena or objects, we draw conclusions that are sometimes diametrically opposed to the point of view of the rest of the society to which you belong. What you take for weakness and call insomnia, for me, is my forte and I call it vigilance. Without it, the downward spiral fall would be inevitable and swift, but we'll talk about that another day, as that's not why I'm wandering around the hotel at this late hour of the night."

Meanwhile, he takes out a tobacco tablet from his pocket and starts chewing it.

"I suppose you've noticed how the city has changed lately?..." he asks looking right through me as if I were transparent.

"Spring has not fully arrived yet." I answer, "It takes a little more time for the vegetation to bloom and for the streets and parks throughout the city to be covered in flowers. However, as soon as you open a window or you get outdoors, your nose is tickled by a sickly-sweet smell. As never before, spring is coming timidly, yet with vernal breeze".

"Again, as always, you do not catch my point. I mean the people. Doesn't it feel like something is brewing in town lately? I smell a lot of turbulence everywhere these days, you know?"

Karl is fond of conspiracies and mystical stories, and the word that's getting around is that he participated in a revolution or two that took place somewhere in Latin America when he was a young man. And, according to wagging tongues, the revolutionary flame is still lit in his bosom. However, I found it easier to believe the Earth is flat than that Karl is a revolutionary fighter. After all, who is that revolutionary who lives away from his revolution? I have heard that the revolution devours its own offspring, but for the revolution to spit them out, that can never happen. He spends his free time with some other paranoid adventurers, with whom he has formed a kind of secret club, where they gather to discuss adrenaline-inducing "coups" to fuel their desires at the sad-boi hours.

"After living here for so long, you ought to ought to have realized by now that if this city is blessed with something like no other on Earth," I say, looking at him straight in the eye, "it is the vibrancy that floods all the way through it, like lava in the mouth of a volcano. There is nothing extraordinary, maybe a few more hormones in the seasonal blood change that return like swallows in the spring, disturbing the dead of winter."

"This remains to be seen. Anyway, to be honest, I've always wondered what keeps me so attached to this place, and now I get it. It reminds me of my golden days when the dice were rolled with the winning chance printed on all six of their faces. These days make me recollect the times when the only things that could be burned and turned to ashes were the monotonous hours and the bachelor's handkerchief." he says excitedly, putting his hand on my shoulder.

"You mean that your biggest effort is the fact that you rolled the dice hard to eject the boredom away?!" I ask him.

"Hope deferred makes the heart sick. Like the snake that sheds its skin, you have to trim the monotony for your heart freshly to leap." Karl almost bursts into verse.

"And I who believed that the snakebite medicine to barbarism was to shoot cannon for freedom!" I return the couplet.

"Even though you aren't that sharp, you're not completely useless. It makes me reflect on myself and many other things that have not occurred to me before." he kills the conversation and, as is his custom, leaves without greeting.

"Maybe it doesn't take much insight to do an autopsy on your thoughts." I answer as I look at his spectral figure crawling behind me.

Meanwhile, I walk forward, enter the office and sit down to prepare the end of the day's reports. Although I have done this who knows how many times, and I have memorized every single procedure by now, puzzlingly tonight the numbers seem too intricate and the ratio of figures too heavy to process in my brain. The data flutters off the report sheet and spreads like hieroglyphic fireworks across the room. It takes me a long time to pick them up one by one from the four corners of the office and then put them together in my description-report mesh.

                              *   *   *

I start to get cotton mouth, the pupil of my eye dilates, and all I can absorb from the sheets spread out on the desk is a pile of irregular spots and lines, signs that convince me it's time for a short break to refresh the mind and renew the strength. I get up, go to the bathroom, and splash a fistful of water, perking myself up. At this moment, the phone rings, and the receptionist informs me about the arrival of Mrs. B. Bekteshi and her acquaintance. Waiting in the middle of the hotel lobby, she hasn't changed a bit. Each time I see her, it dazzles me how the burden of the years has not put any pressure on her physical appearance and her agility to communicate with others. I had a grasp of it since the first time I met her a few years ago. As a ball of fire, she stands in the middle, surrounded by several people whom she guides with numerous requests and agile movements. She asks the receptionist for the same suite she had during her last stay at the hotel, and he assures her that everything is arranged according to her needs. She hands over the suitcases to Ermal, and he departs to carry them to her room. Then, she greets the barman by waving her hand from afar and indicating to him to make two of her usual drinks. He, approving by slightly shaking his head downwards, welcomes her with a smile and sets out to prepare her order. While the security guard hands her some banknotes and coins, which he has just exchanged for local currency in order to pay for the taxi that transported her from the airport, the driver is waiting outside the building to settle the service fee. In that short span of time, the hotel turns into a fortress, and she a princess among her most loyal subjects. As she takes out the cigarette pipe and puts it on her lips, I see her acquaintance, who takes the lighter out of his coat pocket and bending slightly towards her, lights her cigarette. Maybe the tailcoat he's wearing and the Salisbury hat on his head make him look slimmer than he really is, but in any case, he doesn't have a rotund body. His cheekbones are red with no facial hair, and on his crooked nose, he wears round gold-plated glasses. His hair is sparse and greyish, and he must be in his late forties.

She catches sight of me from afar, greets me, and I approach and meet her while returning the greeting with a smile.

"Welcome back, Mrs. Bekteshi! I hope the journey was stress-free and filled with comfortable seats. Is everything going smoothly with the check-in?"

"Ah, dear T., here at the hotel, the service has always been more than perfect! And I always feel one of a kind, as soon as I step in here," she answers me as she lightly takes a drag on her pipe, discharges the smoke and then adds, sighing "but, as for the journey, it was miserable, absolutely on the rack. Wouldn't you agree, Pasqualino?" she addresses her acquaintance, sitting beside her, not taking his eyes off her for a moment.

"That's right, dear. It was a real nightmare." he answers, as he removes his glasses and polishes them by rubbing them with a piece of brown suede fabric.

"I had a bad presentiment as I was standing at the airport terminal. I saw the pilot and his wingmen, the cocks of the walk laughing out loud, while the cabin attendants followed behind, like happy chicks with their heads up. 'What is this great happiness at this hour of the night?!' I thought to myself. Are they off to fly a plane or to enjoy themselves at a masquerade event?! Anyway, we boarded and sat down in our seats. At last, the plane lurched and was getting ready to take off, but though we had been hovering on the runway for over twenty minutes, we were still cruising down at minimum speed and were not getting off the ground. Meanwhile, the pilot informs us on the interphone that the reason for taking so long to take off was that the runway was flooded with snow. And, although another storm was heading our way, according to their calculations, we were safe and sound and would get around it in time! That was a spine-chilling moment as if we were getting ready to go to the netherworld and not on a journey back to our homeland."

"Those words and the pilot's voice were spooky, like the liturgy of a priest during a communion." chimes in her companion for a moment.

"As if all that wasn't enough," Mrs. Bekteshi resumes, without waiting for Pasqualino to finish his last word "someone in the cabin started shouting deliriously. We couldn't tell whether he had cut his wolf loose while taking advantage of the spirits that were sold duty-free at the airport, or if he was seriously ill, or being a little cuckoo. Although I pointed this person out to the flight attendants, they waved their hands and instructed me to sit down and fasten my seat belt because we were about to take off. And so it was; we finally were lifted up in fear and trembling, which pervaded the air in the cabin, with that one man hysterically chattering. The only words I could make out from him were the mutterings that we would crash at any moment and that this would be our last trip."

"Contagious ravishment were his words for all of us." says Pasqualino, "Some started to pray, like I did. Only during the take-off, I must have died multiple times in a row." her voyaging associate intervenes again establishing himself as a person involved in the incident.

She glances at her buddy out of the corner of her eye, smiling, slightly tightening her lips as if to pity him, and then goes on recounting the rest of the events that unfolded during the trip "Well, finally, the plane took off, but right then, we experienced a flight spin when we realized that the passenger in question, in addition to being drunk, was also unrestrainable in his body movements. The situation could turn at any moment into mayhem for all of us who were there. The cabin attendants were afraid to approach him as he twitched and swerved uncontrollably. The pilots were notified rallying a couple of stout men on call and when they realised that there was no way to convince him not to behave in such a way as not to endanger the lives of everyone on the plane, they pinned him down and strapped him to the seat with scotch tape. They even stuffed his mouth so that he wouldn't bother the rest of us with his delirious babbling and moaning. Then, when the situation was brought under control, the pilot informed us that there were two choices for us to consider. Either to fly in circles for an hour, in order to lose enough fuel for the plane to lighten and be able to touch down, since the heavy load prohibited the possibility of an immediate and safe landing. Or else we could continue the journey and hand over the unruly passenger to the authorities at the final destination. Of course, we all preferred to go ahead with our journey, as who knows when another flight would be ready to operate. Moreover, during the time the plane would be wandering around to lose enough fuel, the storm could approach close enough to engulf us in its dominion. But the lack of toilet paper makes it the worst trip I've ever experienced in my life. The flight attendants clearly manifested anxiety about this deficiency in their plane, but still, smiling, they brought us some paper napkins from the service trolley. If they had considered that on the napkin, it was written in capital letters 'At the press of a button, the whole globe is in the palm of your hand', they might have thought twice before handing."

"Truly a slanderous thing!" Pasqualino jumps into the conversation, "I severely reprimanded the attendants and requested that they return at once and be supplied with the correct toilet paper. Where I come from, the toilet is the best-furnished setting because we spend quality time there, and we do not put up with such despicable mistakes."

Meanwhile, the waiter approaches our table to serve the drinks ordered. Mrs. Bekteshi takes this opportunity to inform me, her voice lowered to a whisper, while Pasqualino is exchanging remarks with the waiter about the brand and mixture of the spirits, that he, Pasqualino, as a young boy, had served for some time as a deacon in a monastery with strict requirements for hygiene. Then Mrs. Bekteshi asks us to go and sit because she feels tired and her energies are no longer inexhaustible, as they used to be when she had played her most successful role in the theatre twice on the same night. In those days, spectators had gone frantic with delight, and the world and his wife flocked from the most distant cities, so much so that the hall was packed, like the boats with immigrants when they cross the sea towards the shores of hope. But while the latter were stirred by waves of despair and hunger, the former were stirred by waves of drama and compassion.

In the end, after lodging a formal complaint upon arrival, the airline that had issued the tickets promised to refund them ten per cent of the costs for the unpleasant events during their last trip, as well as upgrade them to VIP class at the cost of economy fare the next time they made a reservation.

"But you, darling, are cooler than the waters of the Pierian Spring and more beautiful than all the bouquets of flowers taken together." Pasqualino tries to make her relax with soothing words, "Your soul, as your complexion, age has not dishevelled even with a single crease."

"Pasqualino, you sweet-baboo," she replies, as she takes off her white gloves, puts them on the table and gently caresses his hand "but I do not deserve your praise for I am a nagging woman, and as fussy as a hen with one chick."

While the two guests are still silently reflecting on the events of the trip, sometimes shrugging their shoulders and twisting their lips, and sometimes shaking their heads and smiling to themselves, I take advantage of a moment when they both fall still and turning toward Pasqualino, I ask him "Forgive me, sir, but you don't quite seem to be from these parts. And yet, you speak our language so fluently, I'd have mistaken you for a native."

"How did you guess that I am not from around here?" Pasqualino reacted surprised to my observation, "After all, I have tried to adapt the accent as best as possible to this beauty, that when I saw her for the first time, 'Whare the heart gaes let the tail follow' I said to myself." says Pasqualino affectedly, turning towards Mrs. Bekteshi gazing at her with sparkling eyes.

"You can say that I was impressed by your refined manners and that rather posh accent. It's different from any other that I have heard before, and the fact that you're such a bang-up cove."

"Pasqualino is of the same seed as us, but he was born and grew up in the diaspora." intervenes Mrs. Bekteshi, "Do you recall how twisted and bitter I was the last time I was gone? More than anything else, what drove me to despair was the lack of sensitivity that people manifested towards subtle beauty and our most precious mores."

"I remember you were crestfallen and so emotionally damaged. During those days when you were getting ready to leave, there was such a cloudburst, as if the sky was about to fall." I answer back to her.

"To recover my vernal self, I went to a town far away. The locals there were rather unlike the people one typically meets, as they never expressed themselves frankly and reached what they were seeking by employing indirect methods based on meticulously concocted plans. Once arrived in that city, misunderstandings were inevitable, as everyone tried not to say what they thought and tried to read the speaker's true intentions between each other's words. I must admit that pleasant surprises did spring out of this oddity in the form of countless improvisations and innovations conveyed while communicating through words and the most diverse expressions.

In the first days I spent there, my deadpan like a heavy act curtain on a long-abandoned theatre stage, the locals perceived it as if I was harbouring a one-of- a-kind that I didn't want to share with the others. Every time I happened to sigh at a bar or restaurant, running my fingers through my hair as I recalled some not so pleasant episodes I had just left behind, the natives turned towards me, assuming that I was signalling to let them know that I was now ready to show what I had been keeping on the sly to myself, so skilfully for so long. And whenever I came face to face with them, by the many cues and gestures as we exchanged glances on the streets, it led me to understand that they were seeking a confession from me, as sooner or later, they would unearth the truth, no matter what. But the only thing I was hiding was the desolate state caused by the melancholia of my unhappy experiences and that I wasn't hiding anything on purpose. For weeks and months, I was as silent as a tombstone, and this made the residents all the more inquisitive, and determined to learn about me and the circumstances of my arrival in their town.

At long last, when all hope of a voluntary confession seemed lost, the local council decided to organize a small festival that was dubbed 'The Silent Stranger's Day', where anyone who was recently visiting the city should by any means march by the vineyard, where they would foottread on bunches and grapes on top of a large wooden vat, performing the vigorous *pigeage*. This festival would symbolize the transitory bridge between the welcoming hearts of the locals and the pleasant conversations and stories wrapped in mystery, which a stranger visiting the city naturally harbours."

"A brilliant idea, wouldn't you say?" Pasqualino picks up the conversation, "It suddenly struck me right between the eyes when I was asked at the council meeting to organize an event to present the customs of our town to foreign visitors." he continues, boasting, " At that time, I hadn't yet met Mrs. Bekteshi, and I was not aware that she was originally from the same country where my great-grandparents came from. Although I had heard something on the grapevine that an enigmatic stranger was hanging around our town and had clouded the minds of many residents with her impressive mannerisms."

"At the gathering, as we were stomping on the freshly harvested grapes with our feet," Mrs. Bekteshi resumes the conversation "I felt the sadness lifted off my chest, and for the first time in ages, a trace of joy found its way onto my face. It was during that, I met Pasqualino, and I found out that a whole community of our diaspora compatriots lived in that city."

"As I saw your shanks, ankles, and calves wine-stained while dancing, holding the hems of the dress with both hands, it fired me with a burning desire to know you." says Pasqualino, not lifting his eyes off her, "Your slender body that leapt up and down, it seemed to me like a butterfly relishing nature, being away with the fairies swinging footloose in the garden of my dreams."

"I remember how you were engaged in venery like a big bad wolf trailing its wounded prey and waiting for the opportunity for it to lose its strength and collapse to the ground." says Mrs. Bekteshi, while a sincere smile dawned on her face.

"If I was guilty of seeking your tumbling down, I'd never let you fall anywhere but into my arms. Although fankled in this chasing, I've yet to understand who is the prey and who is the hunter. If I am the predator, I am indeed a lost cause with no red either in tooth or claw. For such is one when trapped in a time warp of an illusion." says Pasqualino, and in the meantime, he aligns the palms of his hands together and crosses his fingers, rubbing them together.

"That's why we are here, to lift the veil on that illusion." she answers and carries on narrating her story, "Pasqualino was the only human being after a very long time who, perhaps because I sensed something familiar in his face, cheered me up and made me feel safe and outspoken in a conversation with another person. And that town was special indeed. What impressed me the most was the fact that unemployment was zero there, for the reason that all its inhabitants worked their soul-case out decoding the meanings of speeches that were delivered by various officials and politicians. Willy-nilly, during the processing of the passages they listened to, they acquired new vocations in the field of oratory and influencing the masses, as well as persuading the general opinion through mobilizing rhetoric. Of course, not everyone managed to reach the kernel of truth out of a bunch of hogwash. The time it took one to do this varied from individual to individual, but compared to other surrounding cities, they have the highest proportion of citizens stripping the message away from the noisy broadcasting interferences and fully absorbing the essence of its meaning. I was amazed by this phenomenon and have discussed it many times with Pasculino, who, having held a high position in the city administration, understands better than anyone else what I am trying to say. And as such, he can on it far better than I ever could. Or isn't that so, Pasqualino?"

"Yes, this is true." affirms Pasqualin, "Our city is quite special, where, unlike other places, its political and spiritual leaders are aware that it is not easy to interweave the goals and hopes of thousands and millions of people in fact, it is almost impossible. This is because not all people have the same objectives; even if we take it for granted that they have the same life mission or cravings, people cannot agree on how best to pursue them. Moreover, it is impossible for the general masses to find a common language for their hopes and prayers, since from the same expression or idea, due to the differing education and experiences one has had in life, different meaning springs to one's mind, which, in addition to the ones I just mentioned, adds more confusions. These differences in the masses make speaking in public a challenge. As I was saying, all the politicians in my town are on the same page about the basic common good. And this, in essence, is the abolition of common evil, as well as various threats, which may well be internal to the state, such as unemployment and law and order, but also external, for example, threats that may be imposed from a foreign power. Nowadays, these two forms are no longer found in a pure state but often overlap with each other, and as a result, a high level of commitment is required to uncover them. That aside, they are free to compete as to who can better articulate and fulfil the needs of society at large."

Meanwhile, Pasqualino interrupts his speech to moisten his lips with a sip of water, and I seize the moment to ask him to clarify the idea he was trying to convey "You mean the fundamental common good serves as the foundation upon which you build your future?"

"Yes!" answers Pasqualino, stroking the pencil moustache and the sparse hairs on his chin with his fingertips.

"But just now, you mentioned how difficult it is to get people to agree to achieve a common objective. How do your leaders manage to consent on such a vague topic as the fundamental common good, or as you called it, 'the cancellation of the common evil'? I mean, how do you manage to conflate self-interest with clan or class interest and then with that of society as a whole?" I ask him further with great curiosity.

Pasqualino, after gyrating his head and eyes as if he were gazing at the somersaults of a circus acrobat, answers me "First and foremost, a man is initially guided by his own self-interest, and it cannot be otherwise. But a politician with a conscience understands that his personal achievements would not materialize without being based on what are called common customs or values, such as culture or language, without which he would not be able to formulate his personal interest, to begin with, let alone to convey the common good to others. So, a politician is aware that he is a product of this society and owes a debt to make it prosperous, even by sacrificing his own self-interest."

"This is easier said than done. Concretely, how do you achieve this in your city?" I intervene as I knit my eyebrows out of curiosity.

"Initially, a politician accomplished in his career tries to morph what he defines as a personal good to that which belongs to the community. He derives these aspirations or goals from that unselfish act of love, and after doing so, he addresses society at large through public discourses."

"But this will inevitably create dissatisfaction among others who do not think alike." I notice.

"Yes, but he does so with the hope that those 'other few' will be a minority. In times of peace, only elections and the secret ballot determine who shares in most of the common good. Indeed, all sound standings are equally valuable, but there is only one, which is the right one. And it hangs as much on the external as the internal circumstances and conditions of the society." says Pasqualino, and with a handkerchief embroidered with diamonds, which he takes out from the inside pocket of his tailcoat, he wipes beads of sweat that shine on his forehead like dewdrops.

"Since a politician channels the common good by restraining his ego, it means that the basic common good, or the general good, remains ultimately relative and undetermined because the ego can be conditioned up to a certain point, since with its complete annihilation, the subject itself, that is the individual, will be destroyed." I push the conversation forward.

"In a utopian society, there would exist a single super-consciousness, nurtured by associating with all the personal egos of the people in the community. And the only internal or external threats to it would be ignorance of things related to itself, as well as the surrounding environment. But these previously attempted experiments have ended in disasters, as described in the holy books by the Tower of Babel. The numerous and bloody wars and the inhuman dictatorships add more proof to this case. It remains that the best possible arrangement, at least for the time being, is that the same community of citizens has not less than two political groupings that basically share the same goals and basic ideas for the common basic good, but as regarding anything else they are encouraged to nourish their own bearings." answers Pasqualino, occasionally glancing at Mrs. Bekteshi.

Very confused by the concepts he was using, I ask him to elaborate further "Is not the definition of the basic common good as infinitely difficult as that of the general one? Moreover, according to what you are saying, it is equally important that within the same political grouping, there is an opposition, and by the same virtue down to the singular voter, who, in principle, must have at least two competing attitudes towards the same objective, springing from the same premises. But isn't this an abyss of contradiction that breeds schizophrenia, where two different systems of belief and desire are embodied in a single human being?"

"The contradiction fades if you consider that the arguments for a certain concept are always cyclical. As a result, an opposing system of beliefs must share a common source of concept or set of related concepts. Even if they pass via opposite channels, they will have to meet head-to-head sooner or later. In eminent leaders, this intuition comes naturally, you could say almost instinctively. It is built as a defence mechanism against the destructive forces of the past that coerce them to agree on basic principles and the constitutional common good."

"You mean it acts, more or less, like an immune system, when a virus or bacteria threaten it?"

"Yes, that's how it is."

"In relation to new threats, when the basic principles are completely or partially negated, how does this organism react?" I press him further, doubting what he was saying.

"I think that in this case, first of all, you should be careful to mark the cause-effect chain of the events as far as you can. If you are able to connect the dots and make a template of the structure of the 'plague' that hit you, you can use this in the future to prevent the same thing from happening again. As for the first wave of shock, you must bear in mind that whatever knowledge is attained in life cannot be acquired without sacrifice. And, like the ordination of the priest, on the day of the sacramental ceremony, the Holy Spirit permeates his memory to prepare one for the challenges ahead; in the same way, you must hope that with the new knowledge ensued, you can re-erect on top of the old castle's ruins an even more unyielding one, with the same materials and components, but arranged differently."

As he says the last words, his eyes light up like two pieces of hot coal.

"I believe that every castle is as strong as its weakest spot. And the weak spot in the castle that you just described is that it is not immune to dangers it has not faced before."

"How can a castle be immune from an unprecedented danger." he cries, blinking rapidly his eyelids.

"I didn't say anything like that, but to wait for disaster to level the existing one to the ground and then hope you can rebuild everything from scratch seems to me a more painful fatality than the legend of the castle that is erected during the day only to be destroyed at night." I conclude and look at Mrs. Bekteshi, who is contemplating us with sealed lips. And while observing us, deep down, she's feeding her soul with distant thoughts.

"My new friend!" Pasqualino, addresses me, while he is already distracted and has a slight nervous tic on his face, with his eyebrow and eyelid moving, wound up. Meanwhile, his lips waver between a smile and a frown, "How can you have knowledge of anything without first facing it?! Heavenly knowledge was once embodied in a man, the son of God, and the only way it can happen again is when he returns among us. But even He, with His perfection, was not omniscient, since only the almighty God knows when he will return on earth again." declares Pasqualino, and the last words seem to lump in his throat.

"If anybody were omniscient, life would no longer have a meaning." I say to him, "Once when a famous folk maker and rhapsodist was invited to a party organized at the hotel where I work, I asked how he managed to live so freely and unbothered about what tomorrow might bring. He told me it was because he lived under the same roof as the sound. He was convinced that the sound thrilled and pacified even the most violent hearts and shook off with susurration the menacing thoughts of everybody, without exception. Inside him, the sound itself, apart from these features, managed to clarify the mind and transcend many confused thoughts, refining those. And with the help of God, or by pure chance, he conveyed his odes through his larynx, like a flock of storks as they take off from the lake to migrate.

For him, this part did not come about without pain and suffering since whenever he sang, the whole essence of his being had to spring out of nothingness; at the same time, the boundless fear of non-being had to be negated in order to give life to his existential possibilities, freeing the verses from the chains of darkness. I remember him pointing out that every time he sang, it was like the first time. At that moment, the clouds in the sky stood still, and his heart grew heftier until it was torn apart in two by the force of its own weight. And only when a flash of lightning lit up the soul's realm did he burst into song like a raging river overtopping its banks. This was also the reason why he lived so freely, appreciating each day as if it were his last.

If only a sound were enough to penetrate deep into our ignorance, to help us widen the bounds of our knowledge a little more, in this way, the castle would become stronger day by day, without being razed to the ground, since it would completely crumble only in our *de juro* opinions, and thus bring about an improvement of the *de facto* construct." I conclude the sentence that sounded more like a burning desire than a confession.

"How I would like such a sound to attend us now in our conversation." intervenes Mrs. Bekteshi, her face showing signs of impatience, because she is not used to remaining without saying a word for so long.

"Only if you know the truth can you accumulate knowledge. Everything else is all my Eye and Betty Martin." jumps in Pasqualino, as if saying that to convince himself rather than the rest of us.

"Something akin to the story that you just described of the sound and the rhapsode happened to me as well, during the time I visited the town where I met Pasqualino." Mrs. Bekteshi starts to speak with a trembling voice as if she just woke up, "Thoughts of my past failures kept vexing me at all times, pounding like a hammer in a parallel universe, as I tried to recover from my last disappointment." she begins to say, while slowly finding her tongue, "When one day suddenly, all the ablaze fragments of my memories were molten to a single desire. And in this way, I was stricken with an idea. I reasoned that all my efforts were in vain because, although I was very good at piquing the most intimate emotions of the people assembled at the hearings I conducted in support of my causes, I was still unable to appeal appropriately to the popular logic, as well as to the interests of certain classes in the society. During the time I got to know Pasqualino, I was impressed by the ability of the culture there to cultivate cunning politicians, who, through public speeches, realized their personal aims of being appreciated and respected by others. And at the same time, they prospered for the common good. This was thanks to their ability to mix personal growth with that which generally improved the city. And despite being a small town, it had been able to generate politicians of national and international stature far better than any of the surrounding towns. Thus, considering that Pasqualino has been a high-ranking official in the administration, making many connections in the social spheres there, I was hoping that he would help me found a political party here in my hometown to further the aspirations of my people. He will help me to progress where I have previously stumbled. In a few words, with the right approach to the logic of the crowds, or where logic does not do the trick, the message can be absorbed through the unconscious by manipulating the feelings of the entire population. If only you knew how important this mission is to me. If even a single drop of a tear were to drip over the container of my broken dreams, I don't believe that I would be able to handle it, and I would most certainly be a candidate for a laughing academy."

"My turtledove, forget everything that happened to you before, as I shan't let anything on this earth gripe your fragile soul." Pasqualino bursts into the conversation.

"What do you think, T.?" Mrs. Bekteshi asks while looking at me, "How does my endeavour seem to you? Do you reckon it will be successful?"

"To be honest, I don't know what to tell you." I answer, "Here, political organizations and parties have become more numerous than neighbourhood pubs. Everywhere, all talk and no work."

"You see, B., no one understands you the way I do." Pasqualino leaps in her defence, cocking up, "There is no way it can happen otherwise when others interpret your dreams as amounting to a hill of beans, which in reality are like slipping pearls from your eyelashes."

"If I could wrap up the talk, I would say that when the will matches talent, nothing is impossible." I add with tact and diplomacy.

"If your way of supporting our cause is by not letting other people get a word in edgeways, then our dance card is full!" bristles with anger Mrs. Bekteshi, "T. might be the first member of our political party. But if you keep heaping coals of fire in his head, I'm sure he won't have much incentive to jump onboard. Claw me, claw thee. Or am I wrong?!" she brings to an end her chew out by turning toward me and grinning like a Cheshire cat. Her nose like a pea pod, wrinkles slightly resembling that of a tigress. And then facing me she adds "Please T. ignore what Pasqualino says tonight, as it is quite understandable that his natural flow of thoughts is hindered after an exhausting journey."

"You are right, hen." Pasqualino concedes, "We have had a very busy day and an eventful evening so far, and maybe a not so well thought out word or two may have slipped from my tongue, but I do not believe that this bright young thing, that we had the pleasure to meet tonight will have any hard feelings. Moreover, I have been enjoying our feast of reason so far. I hope he doesn't hold a grudge against me."

"Holding a grudge?! That is not a word in my vocabulary." I rush to answer, "On the contrary, I was enjoying the conversation as much as you. It is truly an honour for me to be in your company."

"Excellent then." Mrs. Bekteshi continues, "This means that you could very well be the first member of our political party."

"I'm very grateful for the offer, but I can't accept it." I reply, taken off guard, "Firstly, I don't have the time to engage in such activity. Secondly, I am a sceptical and baffled follower. Neither would your organization gain anything from me."

"Don't worry, T.. For starters, you don't have to be committed to a great extent. You have to attend a meeting or two outside of working hours, which will serve you better to relax and meet new people than of being burdened with any responsibilities or tasks. Therefore, more than your attention and concentration, in our meetings, I need your physical participation." she tells me, and as I am just about to answer her, she quickly adds "In particular, it would be a bad omen for my latest initiative, that the first person I proposed to embrace this movement did not do so."

I already realize that she wouldn't let me off the hook, and any further objection would prove fruitless. So, perforce, I am appointed as the first member of the political party led by Mrs. Bekteshi and Pasqualino, even though I am completely unaware of its ideology or undertaking.

Mission completed, Mrs. Bekteshi lights another cigarette while Pasqualino lights his tobacco pipe, and merrily, like merchants that have sealed a lucrative bargain, clink their glasses and start to talk about the course of action in the coming days.

And as the smoke billows upwards, below rolls the buzz and laughter of our tête-à-têtes, which had already left politics at the door, plunging into the waters of literature, music, and those few magical arts that feed the mind and ease the soul.

A little later, Mrs. Bekteshi stands up, and, unable to stick around any further, wishes us good night and leaves for her quarters.

Pasqualino and I entertain our ideas a little more, which at the shank of the evening could only be fragmented and careless, and we part soon after.

At the crack of dawn, the first flashes of light beam their reflection on the surfaces of the glass panels of the hotel and a pale-yellow light comes slanting in and slides across the floor, sprinkling gold on every corner of the building.

The flow of activities, sporadic until that hour, becomes more frequent until, with the swapping of the personnel at the end of the shift, everything comes to life, and a normal working day on the premises of a hotel begins.

*　　*　　*

The lights of the houses and on the poles still flicker under the morning misty twill that hungs over the city. The roads procreate vehicles in a column, and many people hurry along the sidewalks with puffy eyes and crumpled, sleepy faces. Among them, I stir my stumps, rambling back home. As I move forward, I am thinking about how to surprise Ikun by preparing breakfast or at least getting on her good side by making a cup of coffee especially for her. Meanwhile, I pictured imagery that thrilled me out of my sluggishness, the moment when she would sip and, with a sincere smile, thank me, as she always did, for the perfect coffee I prepared for her, though she would like to have it with less caffeine and lots of milk. All of a sudden, it dawns on me that Ilir has to be informed of what has happened to Besian. So, I decide to swing by his house first to see if he has returned from his last trip. He is the youngest and the apple of the eye of his five sisters since they lost their parents when he was only eighteen years old in a road accident; he was forced to work as a teenager to support the family, leaving his passion for sculpture in the shade for some time. Now that all his sisters were married and settled, he was finally free to devote himself with flesh and soul to art, and not a day passed without him giving it thought, trying to make up for lost time at all costs. His source of income originates from custom work and sculptures and statues he creates, which he sells in various exhibitions. When he is short of money (tell me an artist who has had too much of it!), his sisters never leave him high and dry. His dwelling is a two-story house with a gable roof with cracked tiles here and there, or rather the right half of what's left of a two-story house. This is because the owner of the left side had first tried to convince Ilir to demolish the house and raise a multistorey building on the foundations of the old one. Each time, he passed on the offer since that house was all he had left as a legacy from his parents. He did not have the heart to pull a brick out of it for any profit, let alone tear it down. "And the stroll down memory lane that the house bestows on me, where can I buy it afterwards?" was the first line on his lips as someone presented him with an offer. So now, adjacent to the house where he lives, a huge building is raised, leaving the latter's roof in the shade, like a mushroom at the base of a pine tree. This was not a bad thing in all its twists and turns since the great shadow cast by the building had accelerated the plant growth and invasion of the greenery in all directions, especially the roses, which, with their thorns, always made the entrance from the outer courtyard to the house a challenge.

Meanwhile, the closer I approach his house, the dallier I am getting from fatigue and sleeplessness until finally all my strength is spent and my body begins to sway like a perch, but fortunately, this happens while at the threshold of his door. I lean over and support my shoulder against the wooden door, which creaks open as soon as I touch it. This means he was back from the trip, as the door is always left unlocked when he is in town, regardless of whether he is at home or out and about. I hold on to the handle to keep myself from falling, and shuffling along I manage to get inside. In that condition, as I swing from side to side, I enter the main room of the house and plump down haggardly on the couch.

The perturbed murkiness within the room is, from time to time, brightened by luminous flashes, which, from outside the window, penetrate into the interior and then, as it collides with the hanging glass of the lampshade, trickle all over the room.

Ilir has recently experienced some of the most culminating events in his career as a sculptor. The inauguration of one of his best works, as well as the personal exhibitions that he has organized, have given an indisputable boost to his self-confidence and artistic mastery. Therefore, as the sensitive and meditative lad that he has always been, along with success, he has also acquired more responsibility to justify his achievements so far and to bring innovation thanks to the art he practices with such dedication. I can put money where my mouth is when I say that constant dropping wears away the stone and that Ilir is now entering a phase that most people would call a period of "artistic frenzy". I mean that something has changed in him and his daily routine. It's something that I can't pinpoint, but I can say that he has become more loving and, at the same time, more supple than before.

He wears a pinched face, and during the whole time you talk with him, you notice that apart from having a conversation with you, he is non-stop mulling over something. Furthermore, he does not work with anything other than hard materials, such as marble and stones of all kinds. There is a lot of dust everywhere in the house, and it looks like it hasn't been taken care of in a long time. Only the piano placed next to the porch display stays imposing and glossy, as he polishes it up every day when he is at home. It is also his most beloved musical instrument, even though he knows how to play only a few folk tunes, which his mother taught him as a child. Every time his mother is mentioned, his face is perfused by a wistful grin, as if she is appearing out of thin air. He has so much to say to her, but with a puffed-up chest, he cannot utter a word. He simply smiles and kisses her likeness with his eyes as he blinks his eyelids in slow motion. She had been a well-known composer, and when her slender, nimble fingers glided over the piano playing the keys, the walls of the house shuddered with mesmerizing notes and hypnotic cadences. Those notes made him cease crying and moaning in the crib as a baby. Under those vibrations, he stuttered the word "mama" for the first time, and with the same notes, he took his first steps, swinging. Whenever he thinks about her, or simply when the burnout monotony of the work process suppresses his creative impulse, he sits down at the piano and, enchanted by trooping fairies, plays his favourite tunes or makes some spur-of-the-moment jam. When I look at him in that state, he seems like a virtuous wet nurse gently rocking the memories in the cradle of his soul. Although he loves music to bits, his fingers can only bang out dull noises. But when it comes to creating different shapes or symbols with solid materials, he is a dab hand, exceeding everyone I have ever known. He has the patience of a saint that I believe even the most committed monks would envy. As he says "There is no wood or stone on this earth that I cannot breathe life into thanks to art."

As I collapse on the couch, I call out loud to see if he was home, but I get no reply. Among the many things lying around me, I can spot unfinished and abandoned maquettes, as well as a host of other items and scraps, such as rags, old newspapers, chisels and carving tools, hammers and files of all kinds, as well as stones, rusting steel, rough wood, sand, mud and waste marble blocks. He mainly works in the yard and then stores the sculptures and statues at the back of the house in the garden. As a result, this whole space resembles a huge creative workshop more than a lodging space. While chilling out and looking at the shapes of some of his unfinished works, I notice that one of them is moving. Weary as I am, I thought my vision is working a trick on me, and I rub my eyes to get rid of the stupor. But no, not in the slightest; the supposed statue that I am looking at and which I thought had moved really did do so. And coming towards me is the figure of a fine missy shaped in from the deep, rich-looking gloom of the room. Her willowy body, with fine broad shoulders, is crowned by the sharp features of a fair face, with a small nose and a dimpled chin slightly extended forward. Straight brown hair cut in layers completes her portrait. She halted not far from where I am sitting, and while I am inquisitively looking at her, she addresses me "I'm sorry, I didn't mean to startle you, laddie. You took me by surprise as I didn't notice you coming in. My mind must have been wandering away while I was watching the dust particles floating and sparkling like fireflies in the air." after a short pause, she asks me, "This is so embarrassing. I hope you didn't linger around here for long, have you?"

"Hello! I'm T., and I just arrived." I answer and get up, leaning on the backrest of the sofa, "To tell you the truth, I got quite a bit of a shock by catching sight of you, but now it has turned into a pleasant surprise. And who are you hiding behind those lovely lines of yours?" I ask her.

"My name is Zanfina, and not long ago, I moved with my family into one of the apartments in the building over there." she tells me, and twists her graceful waist, pointing out the window towards her place, "I met Ilir some time ago, and he told me that his door would be open for me whenever I needed it. My dad has left for duty, and having plenty of time to kill, I thought I'd stop by to greet him."

"Ilir has always had a big heart. By the way, is he here?" I ask her.

"No, when I arrived, I didn't find anyone inside." she answers and goes to take a seat on the stool next to the piano, "It would have been nice to have met him, anyway. It is enough to be in this house, and I have the impression that he is everywhere around here, making me feel all the feels. Here, time is experienced like it's just creeping by, not to say that it stops altogether. So all the daily troubles suddenly vanish into thin air, and I become light as a feather."

"I couldn't agree more." I approve of her opinion, "This house is an island of tranquillity, on the shore of which society's gossip crumbles like white foam in a thousand and one letters."

"Exactly how I feel today," she says excitedly "like a survivor washed up ashore by the storm."

"Why? What has happened to you?" I ask her.

"I haven't got the faintest idea why, but this I can only put into words in verse." she tells me, turning toward the piano and starting to sing with the tune accompaniment in the background, "My father is an army brass, and every time he returns from service, his body boils like a volcano. When you talk to him, surprisingly, his voice is husky and alienated. And when you converse with him, he speaks daggers and makes gestures uncontrollably. My mom has tried her best all her life, but she could never get used to his behaviour as another. Now, she stays rugged during the daytime, wrapped in a blanket, and waves at him from afar as he comes and goes to military service. I have never had a problem embracing and smoothing his ruffled feathers and drooling all over his cheeks, while I slide my wet lips onto them. His military march, only I can assuage with my sweet dance. Then I take him by the hand and sit him on the couch, remove his boots and start rubbing his ankles. So, one day, I asked him when I took to wash his liners 'How comes it, dear father, that you are so angry, every time you come back from the service, you blow up?' and he answered me, 'But like the roses with its pointed thorns, pointed lances, my dear daughter, the military uniform hides. It is beautiful and very precious; the blood of heroes for the freedom of the fatherland are inscribed into.'"

Meanwhile, she stops playing the piano and turns to me and says "And when my father is far away, who knows where, I enshrine in my heart the most beautiful memories I have spent with him and relive them when I'm fed up to the back teeth with boredom."

"I was very impressed by the verses you just sang," I sincerely congratulate her for her performance, "and it was a delight to hear the piece of music you accompanied it with. You are such a virtuoso. As two ardent art lovers you and Ilir are, you will surely enjoy chatting with him." I point out.

"I am just amateurish when it comes to art, while Ilir is much more than that. It is enough to look around this place, and you will be convinced of the dedication and skill he works the statues down to the minute detail. For me, art is simply a garnish act, an embellishment, while for him, it is the point where imagination breaks off, and shapes in space and time are formed, only to be congealed back in his thoughts finally. Thus, human life itself with its dramas and comedies."

"I find it hard to believe that you've only just met Ilir," I observe, "because you as though you've known him for a lifetime."

"I expected that you would think so," replies Zanfina, putting a smile on her face, with her snow-white teeth gleaming like the ivory keys of a brand new piano, "but it's not what you think. As I just said, I engage with art in my spare time; nonetheless, I only have to look at the environment someone works in and the excuses they make for their lifestyle to know if they are being single-hearted about it."

"This is a rare skill of yours," I remark in surprise, "considering that no two artists are the same, nor their lifestyles.

"That's true; one might enjoy the nightlife, while another might prefer that of the day," continues Zanfina, "but whatever the propensity, all art creators have something in common. And that is the silence that takes hold of them before commencing their work. The darkest and most impenetrable silence of a night without moon and stars. A silence amassed and compressed deep in the recesses of memory over the years, which suddenly explodes into volume in which everyone, according to his consciousness, tries to give it shape or colour without ever being able to consume it completely. So, for most people, this strange component material is lost when the work takes its final form; for me, it is active and constitutes the essence of the work itself. And I can identify it in seemingly unimportant and often hidden details. A strain of muscles in a sculpture, stress of words in prose or poetry, a little more depth of colour and bending of the lines of an object in a painting, or the flexibility of a soprano's voice in an opera and so on... By the way, this piano needs to be tuned since it emits vaguely dull and muffled sounds." she concludes her speech by playing a few notes on the piano and then listening keenly to the echoing resonances.

"I'm afraid the tuning of that piano is a job that cannot be done," I note, " because Ilir inherited it from his mother and wants to keep it intact from the time she played on it. That aside, I'd say you're a born art critic. Have you been in this profession for a long time?"

"Not at all." Zanfina answers while spinning around the many rings she has on the fingers of her left hand, "I studied architecture, and as a result, I have an exposed nerve about arts in general, especially the visual arts and photography in particular, as they have an internal organic connection with the profession I practice. Like Ilir, I must have an idea or a clear sketch in my head before I start to work to draw the dimensions and delineate an object on a white sheet. This is the space that unites me with the arts in general. However, while I am driven mainly by concepts when I draw, this is not necessarily the case when creating in the field of fine arts because, as I was saying before, in this case, the inner spiritual density drives the creation."

"It seems vocations have been granted to people at birth. Those who are enlightened to legislate and be in charge of affairs due to the formulation of laws and the rest who must follow blindly because obscurantism reigns in their minds." I say in disbelief.

"Please, don't misunderstand me, for I meant not to induce the idea that my work is not affected by my emotional or psychological mood or that the intellect does not come across in artistic works." Zanfina explains further, " On the contrary, if something like this were to happen, we would have two totally irreconcilable organisms with incompatible worldviews, where the first species would have to be embodied with a definition of all measures of the action he had to take throughout his life. And the second species would have to recreate itself every day from scratch, without ever fully actualizing its potentialities, since it would be in a constant state of endless possibilities of existence. In the first case, the species would disappear as soon as it faced an unforeseen danger, while in the second case, we could technically say that it has never existed since its essence would be in a continuous flow, without having the possibility of ever laying the foundations to be actualized. What I want to say is that in the profession I practice, the predetermined structural aspect prevails, which acts as a guideline for my work, while in genuine artistic creations, it is the thought of the unknown and the undiscovered whose call pushes forward to work and create on previously untrodden paths."

"As far as I understand from what you are saying, the class of intellectuals is the most spoilt because they are always illuminated by a mysterious sun. But the artists, in truth, are the chosen of God because, like the Jews, they too are in constant search of the 'Holy Land', although there is a whole desert in-between." I sum up her idea.

"You can say that more or less. But while intellectuals are more cautious of their actions, those who belong to the circle of artists are more vulnerable to external dangers in the natural environment, or the lynching of the social-hysteria.

And I especially brood over young artists because flattery words and congratulations can really feed the ego of their young and innocent souls, giving them the idea that the whole world revolves around them. And so far, there is nothing wrong because in the works which inspire us, and for which they are so much appreciated, it is their world that appears as an idea or a symbol, somehow modifying our own, causing it to lose its normal gravity for a few moments, and to revolve around another star. As a result, the artist fully deserves to think for a few moments that he is the navel of the 'world'. But what I fear most is the excessive blandishment of the masses while planting a false sense of reality in the unconscious, casting a veil of illusions over it that is doomed to bring forth disappointments, along with the harsh and insidious assessment of some nitpicker obliterated by time, which seeks to forge in the abode of those free souls the chains of weakness and hopelessness."

"What you just said is too abstract for me. I'm afraid that this kind of pressure, which you just described, is a skull-buster and may well blow one's brains out." I tease her without any ill intentions.

"There is a grain of truth in every joke." Zanfina tells me with a sullen face, "Otherwise, how can anything new be born without first dissolving the old-fashioned bonds and worn-out points of view, which little by little turn into suffocating fetters of slavery?"

"I completely agree with you," I try to lift her mood with soothing words, "but the only thing that comes to my mind, and that worries me, is the fact that when logic breaks down, or in other words, when meaning whirls around the corroding vortex of the fertility well, the truth might easily be covered by a false face or likeness."

"And yes, that requires wits! Brain and brawn together. Perhaps not a brain tossed about by raging winds, but a subtle mind nurtured and supported by a great heart, which aims to tear off the mask of insanity and thus release the inexhaustible powers restrained until a little while ago in the name of customs or general populist logic. Or rather, I should say the prejudices and the views conceived by a rusty and obsolete logic. Everybody's voices that traverse the collective heavens encapsulated as no body's empty 'thought'. Therefore, a phantom shell that haunts and conceals the creation of anything new in thought." Zanfina answers me, taking out a thin emery board from her pocket and starting to sharpen her nails.

"If that doesn't work well enough, you've got plenty of files lying around here." I try to lighten the atmosphere with a facetious remark, "Still, there is something that I am not able to grasp," I add hastily, "because, according to what you are saying, this mask cannot be torn apart without being involved in this foolish play. Thus, it means that it can only be mauled by a power of greater folly than the one which is lacerating. In this assault, the truth always remains a prey to absurdity. Then the question is how to get out of this vicious circle of madness?"

"First of all, you should keep in mind that the immense light of the truth can blind one. And, being close to the bone obscures the view, and one cannot discern anything, just like the cloudy night that hides the stars." she explains to me further, "As such, it is absolutely logical and necessary for a mask to serve as a foundation to protect one from the beaming truth. At the same time, the logic that serves this end is a thought cured of the nonsense and empty words of the time. It is curated by none other than the rays of infinity, although a definition of infinity is itself impossible, as the temporary mask that the truth wears. You may have a sense of the infinite, but it is impossible to define it."

"Accordingly, what you are saying is that logic is nothing but a temporary lunacy, necessary to protect yourself from the enlightening infinity of truth and a cock-and-bull story?" I ask her, feeling overwhelmed.

"Oh no! If logic were insaneness, it would be like endless chatter without expressing any thought. Rather, logic is infinity itself vested in human garments." she says, and for a few moments, she becomes a shadow of herself.

"Now, without a doubt, all this has gone over my head. If this mask is infinity itself, then what is madness doing in between?"

"Just like the vastness escapes any definition, so does the nothingness. Because if nothing could be defined, then it would no longer be nothing, but something. Isn't it?! Consequently, from this angle, they are the same, but this does not mean they are equal or identical. Absurdity is the very contradiction in which the infinite seeks to explode whatever confines we try to arrange for it by means of logic.

Moreover, only by means of nothingness can infinity leap out of itself so that we can vocalize a new object, concept or idea. So, logic is nothing but infinity condensed into nothingness. A universality that would remain true even if nothingness reigned."

"Then reason is nothing but the mirror where eternity combs her hair!" I conclude firmly.

"Reason is the 'magic eye'," Zanfina puts the last touches on my words "where through the reflection of infinity, everyone is encouraged to conceive definitions on the logic of how different individuals forge interpersonal relationships, and the multitude of these connections, as well as how society interacts in general with the environment where it lives."

"If it is as you claim, then it follows that reason is the agency where our worldviews can be linked into one so that what is outdated can be melted down to forge a new worldview, and this could not have happened if the presence of the infinite did not ripple beside it. This presence is as necessary as it is distant since it is never directly tangible. As such, in a way, hidden and inaccessible. Herein lies the trick: how can we unshackle the infinity within us from the abyss of nothingness in which we plunge it?"

"Ah, that's simple." Zanfina answers brightly, "By means of a frenzied spin, with all your might, you must tear up the mask that covers it in order to release the spores of the truth."

" I," Zanfina continues and starts to walk around the sofa where I was lying, "at most can chant to the birds of the forest and the timid creatures that graze in the surrounding lawns." In the meantime, her hectic whirl starts birling around me, so much so that in the end, the only thing I can catch a glimpse of is the white silky flounce of her dress fluttering behind.

"With my nails, I can poke the fire of a childish delight and steal a smile, but you can only cling to the truth with eagle's claws and eyes." These were the last words I heard from her before she left the same way as she had appeared like a sedating vision of a mountain spring.

Promptly, everything around me starts to fade, and my eyelids get heavy. I already feel my body light as if in a free fall, and yet, only a moment ago, I was completely exhausted and felt sick to my stomach. Hollow sounds rumble from the depths of my being, and bits and pieces of conversations from earlier in the day rise to the surface of my conscience. Although I can't make out the mouths that utter the phrases or remember to whom they belong, the words are clear and unambiguous. Fragmented thoughts branch out and proliferate by means of the dreamer's rope swing and seek to lure me through their endless spaces. I feel my being getting as light as a feather, like a space rocket boosting above the earth's atmosphere, leaving behind everything heavy and uncouth. Sleep has already sprouted its wings on my back, leading me through terrain off the beaten path.

If someone were to ask me to define tranquillity and peace of mind, I would answer that tranquillity is like a particle of light that strikes the surface of water and then strives to penetrate it as deep down within as possible. Like a blazing star that journeys solo through the planetary spaces, radiating behind bright cone-shaped protrusions. Or like a sip of a flavoured and aged cognac on a memorable day. And while I was conjuring up other definitions in my mind, a thundering noise reached my ears, at first as a distant and stifled sound, growing louder and louder, until at last, dry and harsh blows drew my attention and cut the sleeping cord that I was relishing with such gusto. Since I slept like a log, vagueness and confusion still hovered over my head. I can't make out where I am or whether it is the dawn or sunset rays that are streaming in through the window. The uproar that brought me to my senses and kept clanging in the background is Ilir's chisel as it planes the marble slab while hammering away. The rasping sounds he is making transposes me somewhere else, in the middle of an old bazaar, where various artisans diligently practice their crafts and where life always thrives. Unhurriedly, I walk out to the back porch of the house, looking at Ilir as he is in the mix. His appearance has changed a lot. His jaws are expanded, his entire body contracts, and his muscles overexert every time he pounds the chisel. He is wearing his usual black trackie bottoms and a white short-sleeved T-shirt. His long, honey-coloured curly hair arches over his broad forehead and falls loosely over his shoulders. And, from a distance, watching him work gives you the impression that he is grappling with someone in the old-fashioned art of wrestling. Just as in those former times, while the wrestlers exercised and fought under the scorching sun, sweat mingled with the muddy earth, and faces and half-naked bodies scraped on the ground, Ilir is dusted from head to foot, and scraps of skin could be seen between the tips of his fingers, caused by the friction between his fingers and the chisel. The block of marble stood firm in front of him, but even so unyielding stood Ilir as he kept plugging away at the shape he had framed in his mind. A fierce war took place on every square millimeter of the block's surface, "alley by alley, house by house", with marble shards, dust and sweat swirling all over the place. Right now, it's incredibly difficult to pick a winner, as everything hangs in the balance. Each line that the chisel tip etches seems like a path opening up out of nowhere and like a vein by which the parts of the whole will be connected.

For a moment, he stops thrusting the chisel, takes a can of water, and sprinkles the block of marble inch by inch with it to see if any cracks have formed on its surface so that he can mend it without deepening it any further. Satisfied, he spots me as I am looking at him and, smiling he waves and comes over, puts down his sledgehammer, wipes his hands on his trousers and throws his arms around me.

"Finally, your lids fluttered open." he tells me as he squeezes my head between his rough and dusty palms,

"You had started the engines! Snoring so loudly, I was sure you wouldn't wake up until tomorrow morning. Not to mention twitching, flexing and jerking every limb. You were so restless."

"Well, the third shift takes its toll." I answer.

"I know what you mean; it's not the first time I've found you curled up on the sofa. I've always told you the night is made either to rest or to have fun," and he adds, " but anyway, it's important that you have slept soundly."

"It was quite a power nap, and if there were no bang and splat and clap noises, there is a good chance that I would be floating on sleepy waters till sunrise. What about you, when did you come back? How come no word??" I ask him further.

He drops his long hands down and, staring at me, says "I've just been back a few days ago, and right away, I rolled up my sleeves as I had a buttload of work to do. In fact, no one knows that I am back, and you are the first person visiting me."

"Really?!" I raise a brow, "What about those lasses that rush back and forth, with the door barely opening and closing properly? Or do they fall in the bacchante category?" I ask as I wink at him.

"What on earth are you talking about? I don't understand you?!" he turns to me, confused.

"Is this a practical joke?" I tell him, chuckling, "Today, when I arrived here this morning, I found a girl with turquoise eyes and rosebud lips, a rare beauty, like a May breeze, whose name was Zanfina."

"This name doesn't ring a bell to me." he answers calmly, looking around the yard.

"To tell you the truth, I am very surprised since, if you have ever met her, you cannot easily forget her graces, as if outlined by the hand of a painter. And if you add to that the hearty and very pleasant conversation that poured so naturally from her soul, there is no way of getting her out of your head."

"Well, not every wind that blows across a mountain range can bend the tree tops." He tells me, smiling, and goes to the pantry, which is located in the alcove of the kitchen. He pulls a cork there and returns with a pot of wine and two glasses in his hands.

"How was your last trip?" I ask him while we sit on the wooden benches outside.

"It went fine, thank you. I managed to sell two of my latest works and harvest many compliments about the rest. There goes the toast. Here's mud on your eye!" he answers me and raises his arm to cin cin the glasses.

"I'm really happy for you, nonetheless, I am surprised that you haven't found any free time to enjoy the fruits of your recent success either or to meet old mates." drawing his attention once again as the glasses clink.

"Believe me when I say that I'm just swamped these days and had no time at all." he tells me and pauses for a moment while swirling a sip of wine in his mouth, enjoying it to the fullest, "Something unusual happened to me during my time at the exhibition." he continues.

"I would be more surprised if nothing happened there." I note and add, "After all, joint exhibitions are held so that different artists have the opportunity to meet and share their efforts and crafts with each other."

"It is true, but this time, something happened to me that I had not experienced before. As always, I am used to people flocking to exhibitions with the inspiration fever of a spring day, and I look forward to their thoughts and impressions regarding my works.

But this time, I had an unusual visit." he says, avoiding looking directly at me while recalling what had happened during his trip, and carries on, "It may be the case that one may ask me to do custom work for them. Somebody might elaborate on his idea in words, while another shows me the desired object in a picture. But this man who came to see me was different from everyone I had ever met in my life. From the way he walked tall, dressed in a long black overcoat, snowy-haired and a kind-hearted face, he acted as if he had sprung from the arctic glaciers, and there was not a single person around beside him. After telling me how much he appreciated my craft, he asked me if I was interested in creating a work of art for him. Of course, I was extremely excited to accept it forthwith. Then I asked him if he had anything in particular in mind that I could model for him. And here the wonder begins! He wanted me to be the one to choose the model I would work on. And I was lost, for sure, because I generally have a hard time deciding on the next work without having a specific sample to work on. And whenever I've taken the initiative to create something, as soon as it crosses my mind, I've always started one thing and ended up doing something entirely different. And in between, I complete a series of intermediate works. But in this case, I was asked to do a single piece of work; meanwhile, I wasn't sure if what I would end up creating would suit the stranger's taste. Therefore, I asked him to give me his word that he would accept without further ado what I would make, whatever the final product. He said to me in a harsh voice, frowning 'I would accept even a single flower that has its roots deeply embedded in the earth, rather than all the gold mines in this world.

And he stretched his arm, and we shook hands. With that firm, silent handshake, we sealed the deal and parted our ways. Even before the warmth of that handshake faded, as I was piecing together what had just happened, I had a distant and vague feeling that the same thing had occurred to me before. Some phantom soaked my memory as if by a wave. And suddenly, my grandfather's face on the day of my parents' funeral flashed before my eyes. Ugh, how sudden and devastating that accident was... the darkest day of my life." Ilir sighs, and with his gaze fixed, he is lost for a few moments somewhere in the tropical greenery of the yard.

"And not only for you," I try to comfort him, " but everyone who had at least a thread of acquaintance with your parents was sorrowful about what happened! As for myself, I was completely shocked. It happened so unexpectedly. I can't even imagine what it may have been like for you and your close relatives."

"I never again have experienced a more horrible time." Ilir says vehemently, " The first few days, I felt as if I had been tossed into the middle of the ocean. All kinds of people floated nearby to comfort me, but the words that came out of their mouths were choked sounds in my ears, and I could not make any sense out of them. Similar to trying to utter words underwater. But the only thing one can produce is empty air bubbles, which burst as soon as they reach the surface. Although that period remains hazy in my memory and crumpled like a wet ball of paper, my grandfather's eyes, as they looked thoughtfully at me, have not faded even to this day. Relatives on my father's side have always been conservative and taciturn. And among each other, they at most shared a random visit. When they met, while sitting in silence, they exchanged more tobacco than words with each other. Of course, you had to drag the words from my father's mouth, too, and my conversations with him were always consumed in haste. In fact, all the relatives from my father's side are very polite and decent but emotionally inaccessible, with each one living in their own skin and minding their own business. And, as I was saying, my grandfather's eyes left an unforgettable impression on me. He was old and battered by the sudden death. Of course, experiencing the loss of a child, especially your only son, is as if the earth had swallowed up a part of you once and for all. And a black hole is created in your heart, which keeps getting bigger until it devours your entire being. But besides the way he looked at me, something else saddened him as much as the loss of his son. I believe the burden that I had to carry on my shoulders from that day on worried him the most. It was the sheer weight of existence for my still tender joints. And I remember, as our eyes crossed, I had the feeling that a silent conversation took place. And a silent oath bound us inextricably. Well, I had the very same feeling that day when I met the stranger at the exhibition."

"What about his name? What was it?" I intervene, "Was he speaking on his own behalf, or was he representing someone else?"

"I can't say for sure. He showed up out of nowhere, and just as quickly, he vanished, giving me no time to ask him about that. But for the brief moments I met him, we agreed that he would transfer half of the fee for my work into my bank account and contact me another day for further instructions. Yesterday, when I went to the bank, the teller told me that my account had been credited. There is enough for me to live for a year as a god on laurels." he tells me pensively.

"Ambrosia is not a food for everyone to relish." I tease him, "As far as I can see, you have taken too much responsibility for this job."

"You bet I have. You're dern tootin'." he answers me, "From the day that I received the notification from the bank that the money was credited, I withdrew an amount and went with the speed of lightning to the quay of the port in the city of D., to select the marble block on which I would work. Among many slabs standing, this block caught my eye due to its whiteness and smooth surface. At the time I set my eyes on it, I fell hook, line, and sinker. I was so involved in working on it that I didn't know if I was the one creating with that block of marble or if that block of marble was working on and alienating me."

"That you have changed, I can see that," I address him while emptying the glass of wine into my gullet, "but I still can discern the Ilir that I once knew. Take care of yourself, and don't become a total stranger because I wouldn't have any desire to belt the grape and bare my soul with an old pal I didn't know anymore."

"Oh, please. You can't talk yourself out of anything. You can even lay the Ghost of the old town castle at rest." he turns to me laughing and adds, "Do you remember when we were kids and flew our kites high to make brotherhood with the heavens, while as happy as clams laying on the lawns next to each other, inhaling the clouds?"

"Of course," I answer, "he is exactly my friend I used to know, and I wouldn't want you to solidify him into a nameless thing."

"Those were golden times." he continues, putting his hand in his pocket as if he wasn't listening to what I just said, "Everything was easy, and we were only thinking about our next adventure. But after the death of my parents, I started to face hardship and recognized the uncertain and distant aspects of life. Little by little, I started to appreciate those. Now, the only things I can't stand are the easy-peasy stuff, which don't require dedication and sweat because they lead you down a dead-end or head you straight down a cliff. Get me straight; there is nothing wrong with lying carefree for a few moments in the swing of the imagination, crafting up games, or singing serenades under the window. In fact, life would be unbearable without such moments. But you have to make sure that keeping the pot boiling does not turn into a boiling frog. Now I enjoy only those works that stir up the blood and boggle one's mind. I like the hard stuff, but to be hard doesn't mean that they have to be complicated. On the contrary, the simplest things, which are always in front of our eyes, also require more effort to understand. How much of this world that appears before us is created, and how much is made by human effort? Who can say? After all, is there anything more difficult than having but one desire or one goal in life?! Think how exciting that moment was when, according to the myth, Prometheus snatched the fire from the gods in heaven and brought it to mankind. Taking into account beforehand the suffering that he would undergo as a result of the action he was about to perform, he chose to oppose the gods, for he valued the crumbs and troubles of the common people more than the lulling glory of the gods. Many others have done the same in different epochs. They have given up solving the riddles of the universe or astronomy and have dealt with the concerns and issues of people on Earth. Isn't the discovery of electric current in the wake of the same Promethean heritage?! Once upon a time, the stars winked away and pierced the heavens while people danced and gave thanks to the gods. Nowadays, the yellow bulbs on the street's pillars and on every ceiling at homes are the ones that pierce the obscurity and the darkness."

"To tell you the truth, with all this block of marble I see here, your case seems to me more like that of Sisyphus, who pushed the huge stone up the hill, for it only to roll back down again as soon as he reached the top." I throw a teasing remark at him.

In the meantime, he doesn't answer me but holds his silence for a few moments, and his face starts to glow, like the lambent light of a mountain's slope covered with snow, when the first rays of the sun fall on it.

"I just saw you while you were working, and I couldn't understand where the marble block ended and where you began. You had become one body. Have you decided what you will create with it, or are you still in the phase of ploughing on the idea?" I inquire with lots of curiosity.

"Better not ask me about that." he answers, " It's one of the most challenging tasks I've ever had to do. For now, I was just rounding a few corners and polishing off the thin layer of slime and mould that usually covers its surface, especially when it has travelled from across the ocean. In short, I haven't fully started working on it yet. Until yesterday, I had something vague in mind, and I was trying to put some flesh on that, but it was not easy for me because several symbols, shapes, and figures came to me at once. And I am very unsure which one to pick to develop further. I found it almost impossible to decide because all these images that appear before my mind's eye are of equal footing in my heart, and a part of me seeks to bring all of it to existence despite the countless patterns. So, for each sketching idea that I imagine, I create a clay mould and then place it in the hall. All this time, I was in a state of anxiety that made my blood boil, and I could feel the pressure coursing through my veins until last night's dramatic turn of events."

"I feel your agitation, and so far, there is nothing to worry about." I affirm, "You have always had the ability to convey your emotions to others like no one else. I am confident that you will make the right choice no matter what your final selection is going to be. After all, you have done this very same thing since we were little. In difficult moments, you were always the one who instructed us to weigh our actions before carrying them out."

"You might be right, but I never felt like this before." he answers me unequivocally, "From the day of the exhibition, I have been under the sway of spiritual distress, so much so it seems to me that I have to strain my bit of shut eye through a sieve. By the way, if you look carefully over the past two weeks, I managed to sleep only a few days like a log. The rest of the nights, even when I had a chance to doze a little, I always saw the same dream.

I imagined that I was in a meadow at the foot of a mountain, and everything around me was perfect. Clear and enchanting sky, as it usually is in the mornings after a night of downpours and lightning. The cascades from the mountain let their water drop with burbles and splashes over the steep rocks. Then, the spume is slowly dispersed in concentrated waves along the river's course. Everywhere, there are herds of animals grazing, and flocks of birds swirl through the air, releasing relaxing chirps, while I, lying far-stretched on the grassland, without the slightest worry in my mind. In short, heaven itself. The only thing that makes this picture odd is the fact that no trees grow on this mountain, but instead, forests of stones of all kinds shoot tips, from granite, slate, marble, pebbles, stones without pebbles, whin-stone, stones with different colours, that is, all the types of stones that this earth possesses.

Moreover, a few of those stand broken, like the trunks of trees that are split in half and fallen because of their own weight or the violent storms. Between the cracks, you could see rings indicating their age. Naturally, stones cannot be missing in a sculptor's dream." Ilir says, laughing at the ironic self-satire, and after taking a sip of wine, continues, "But this state of comfort does not last long. Suddenly, the sky is turned into a reddish colour, as if it has been sprinkled with the blood of a freshly sacrificed ram. In an instant, a wildfire bursts forth from all four sides. I no longer have the body shape of a human being, but I have turned into a she-wolf that rushes as fast as possible to the den, at her cubs, surrounded by the flames. Chaos and fear reign everywhere around. And, as every living thing rushes against me, I push forward against the stream to get as quickly as possible to my cubs. As I approach the den, I see that the flames have come very close to it, and I only have time to grab one of the little ones by the scruff of the neck and carry it out of danger.

This conditional situation cannot fail to drive me into dreadful despair and indecision since I am compassionate to all my puppies equally... at this point, every night, I wake up sweating and with dry lips, muttering and gnashing my teeth until dawn. All day afterwards, I brood over this event in my mind and, in the meantime, add a new clay model to the antechamber. But while I had the same dream last night, the ending took an unexpected turn. At the moment when I was in front of the den, my heart was pounding like crazy because of the cruel choice of which of the cubs I was going to pick to save, a choice that would have deranging and soul-crushing consequences in any case, a voice that was howling beyond, in the middle of the forest, guided the she-wolf's instinct to select the healthiest, and most indomitable of the cubs from the consuming flames. At that moment, I woke up, as always, bloodcurdling and my hair standing on end. As I went to quench my thirst with a glass of water, I noticed that the clay models I kept in the hall were pulverised. All of them were smashed to pieces, except one, which remained untouched. At first, I suspected that a petty thief or a homeless person had entered the house while I was sleeping, causing the havoc, but I had my doubts because it seemed unusual that all this had happened right next to me, under my nose, and I had not noticed a thing. Considering my light sleep, especially these last two weeks, this seemed quite impossible to me. So, in the end, while not having any new ideas in mind, I decided to work on this model that had survived a dark and obscure night."

"And what is the mould you are going to work on? Can you show it to me? Because after what you just told me, I'm eager to know." I intervened as soon as he finished this part of the narration, which made me fall deep into thought.

"I'm sorry, but what you are asking me for is a thing that cannot be done. I am superstitious about revealing the idea without giving its final form in stone. I promise you will be the first I will show it to once I have given it the general shape." he tells me and raises the wine glass to make a toast.

As I was getting ready to raise my glass, I thought of Besian and the reason I had come to Ilir's house early in the morning. I put the glass down and started to break the news to him "At least you have the luxury of waking up in your home when you are having a bad dream. But Besian is not this lucky, although I'm sure his dreams are many times more terrible than yours."

"Why, what are you implying? What is going on? Tell me." Ilir asks, surprised and extremely agitated. While I tell him everything that happened, I see his face turn yellow, his lips contort, and his eyebrows lean against each other and merge into one.

Every sentence I utter he accompanies with a groan and the expressions "Don't!" or "What are you talking about!", which seem to rumble from the depths of his chest. Finally, I also show him the missive that Besian had sent me, which I had with me, and I see him grief-stricken. His eyes are bloodshot like red pomegranates, but he still holds his nerve and doesn't shed a single tear.

"This is terrible." he addresses me, "I can't find words to describe it. Where is he now?"

"In the 'Tree-hollow of the Lost'."

That's what we call the high-security lockup, located just a few hundred meters from the city centre, which in the previous regime had served as a place of torture against its political opponents. In reality, it was a dark hole lined on all four sides with high, damp, ash-coloured walls. There is also a police station beside it. When I was a kid, I always passed there since it is not far from where I live, and I remember women dressed in black would gather around it, looking for their sons, who had disappeared. At that time, it was common sense that if someone was declared missing, and the authorities did not give any further explanations about their whereabouts, then they would inevitably be either in one of the cells of this prison, being questioned by the authorities, or, if they had their guardian angel watching over them, they would have crossed the border into exile. The chances for the second scenario were rather slim, so the mothers were always prepared for the worst. Just a grave where they could perform a death wail ritual for their boys was all that they were hoping for. I don't know if it was a mere coincidence or concocted on purpose, but across from this prison is the elementary school that I attended, which, ironically, is named after a Renaissance poet. In the lesson, they recited and sang verses about freedom, while a little further from there, free people were sacrificed, a bloody tribute, and a bleeding wound in every civilization. While we in the school-banks, using verses, trying to knit our future, others lingered in the dungeons, life and limbs in shackles, each day slaying over again, everything that life pierces through. In the end, they were left with an empty and meaningless cavity that they called a body. When I think about it today, I don't understand why two such buildings were next to each other. Perhaps some mischievous mind intended for the children to grow up with the cold, damp walls of horror to feed deep in their unconscious, as a memorial to those who dared to wander outside the orbit of the system and its sun, which had to draw around itself, by hook or by crook, all the other heavenly bodies. The prisoners in their isolation rooms had to tear their hearts out as they squealed with joy when they heard our playful voices having fun in between the lesson breaks. I remember our classroom was on the third floor, with windows at the back of the school, from where we could glimpse parts of the prison building. We never saw the shadow of any of the prisoners, and on very few occasions, we saw any of the guards as they changed shifts at the towers. One could not hear a dicky bird and a stony silence reigned most of the time. In addition to the concrete forms and wire meshes that covered the surrounding space, several one-storey houses also served as a dividing line between the school and the prison. The yards of these houses were planted with khaki trees. I remember how we would gaze for hours during the winter at their bright orange fruits on the leafless branches while imagining the stifled, silent moans and groans of the inmates. Perhaps one of the things in common between the prisoners and the poet, whose name my elementary school bears, is the echoes of their voices that remain unanswered. Although nowadays, the violence and systematic torture by the command in the prisons has stopped, the shadows of the past still crawl through the bars of the prison windows. It can still be felt when the cell doors creak and scratch as they open and close or from the stories of the veteran jailbirds.

"Good grief! Haven't they found another place? But instead, they had to lock him in a high-security prison, as if they are investigating the murder of the century!" exclaims Ilir with a contemptuous face, "And when you think that justice should be blind!"

"In this country, if you don't spray golden dust to someone's face, in order to turn a blind eye, they won't even lift a finger." I murmur with a sigh.

Worriedly, Ilir starts pacing around the yard, and every now and then, while muttering something between his teeth, he turns, asking me for further details. He is quite aware that Besian could get carried away sometimes, but this was not due to any sense of superiority he had but simply because he was passionately immersed in discussions that contained contradictory statements about the same subject. He simply required that the interlocutor with whom he was having a conversation, in addition to his own opinion, at least respect the opinion of another if he could not accept it. But this was an impossible task when faced with a mind as closed as an isolation room, a mind terrified by the fact that life might be raging elsewhere independently, beyond their world, and over which they have no control. It was this that tormented Besian unceasingly. As impetuous as he was in conversation, he matched that in being sensitive and quick to apologise if he ever overstepped someone else's bounds of ethics.

"And what harsher punishment can the law pronounce on one who is a judge, jury, and executioner to his hotheadedness?!" Ilir speaks as he roams about, addressing those words to himself rather than to me, "Moreover, what sentence can be served by a justice that weighs the cases according to the zeros the parties have in their bank accounts? According to this logic, someone with fewer zeros would pay higher interest for the redemption of his wrongdoing, for the same typology of criminal offence than someone better off. Meanwhile, the one who is penniless would be sentenced to death for the most trivial crime, as they would declare him bankrupt. But this is madness. It doesn't make any sense whatsoever. If we all breathe the same air on this earth when we are born, why should we be weighed with different steelyard for the same deed?"

The questions were unending. The answers were also hard, if not impossible. Consequently, it was easier to answer those with a new question. Time stood still as our eyes met, and neither of us said a word. Ilir starts to pace faster back and forth on the porch, huffing and puffing occasionally like a steamship. For a moment, he goes down the corridor and, after several consecutive phone calls, seems convinced by the guarantee he received from his cronies on the other side of the line, who had acquaintances and were able to pull a few strings in the apparatus of the prison administration or the prosecution office, that they would do their best to transfer Besian to another security prison, where, among other things, he would have the opportunity to receive conjugal visits from his fiancé. As soon as he hung up, he came and sat next to me, breathing a sigh of relief, freed somewhat from the fraught anxiety. We were then rattling away about everyday stuff.

After a brief time, he told me that he must visit Besian's house to meet his mother and comfort her, and we both left the premises. After we split at the corner of the alley, I quietly make my way to my den.

Outside, it is completely dark, and from the yellowish light emitted by the lampposts, you can see that a thin veil of mist has been cast over on the surrounding fields, next to the road, that buries the area. The eye, gaping around, is watered by the curiosity of whether, behind the foggy curtain that nature has hung down, there lies a prosperous harbour or steep rocks that seek to bite every boat passing by.

*　　*　　*

proverb says that it takes a village to raise a child. At the same time, the guiding light is the angel in the house, which makes it a home. As the riff that I heard sung in Ilir's house when his parents were still alive, since his mother had composed the tune of the song, goes "The heart beats night and day, trembling the soul, and together on the same path with the mind are witnesses to the home, where love dwells." in the same way, my feet, as if they had a built-in location tracking system, lead me to the front door of my lodging, while my mind wanders from sea to shining sea.

It is a three-story house that the owner has cleverly repurposed to let the rooms out for rent.

The kitchen and the living room, one bathroom for each floor, and the corridors are the common spaces I have to share with the other tenants. On the first floor lives a chubby woman who works as a caretaker in the kindergarten, and in the next room, Behar, the homeless man, whom, in a way, it can be said that I and Ikun have adopted, since we are the only ones who look after him.

Both Ikun and I live on the second floor, while on the third floor is a young man freshly employed in government administration. However, from what I observe, he will have a long career there. I say this because I see him standing with his wrinkle-free shirt on even after working hours, and the whole time, he keeps a frozen posture and an ironed smile on his face. All in all, it is an ordinary house, among a series of similar houses, in a neighbourhood on the outskirts of the city, near a university.

As I arrive at the front of the house and I am about to unlock the door, a couple of droplets of water hit the window rail shed and splash me on my left. I look up and see a few lines hanging in Ikun's window to dry. The light in her room is switched off, and most likely, Ikun is in the kitchen preparing dinner. I rush inside, and as I close the door and turn around, I feel something tap me on the back. It is the stick of the mop that Violet had left unattended, which was piercing me behind. I was unprepared for this backstabbing, and even less was I expecting it from her, the person we residents have hired to take care of the common areas, because it's easier for us to agree to build a rocket to go to the moon than whose turn it is to bottom the house.

Violeta is a lively and resourceful middle-aged woman, and despite the huge age difference between us, we who live here have managed to build open and honest communication with her. With a round face, small brown eyes, short eyelashes and messy sticking-up flame-shaped hair, what impresses one the most about her is the natural smile stamped on her face. It is a special grin because it is composed of something combining the silly frankness and the love and obedience that dogs generally have for their masters.

With a stubby stature, swollen legs and puffy arms, always wearing a blue apron pierced by a thousand and one safety pins, she is carried away with her job, so much so that when she is at the peak of her vigour, scraping dirt off the floor, she works like the Dickens. Viola, as we call her for short, had just finished dusting in the living room Meanwhile, she returns to the corridor absentmindedly and quails as she sees me standing as a shadow at the end of the semi-darkened corridor, remaining with her jaws in her lap briefly.

"Darn it all to darnation! You made my blood run cold, you devilish creature!" she gasps, putting her right hand lightly on her chest, "Even the snake doesn't terrify his prey like this."

"I know I have this effect on people, especially when they try to 'stab me in the back'." I answer in a friendly tone, "Why is this mop here, right next to the front door? You know very well that exits must be kept free at all times, especially the main ones. Because you never know when there may be an urgent need to rush out the door in a heartbeat."

"The only case of urgency that can happen here is for me to get out of sight at once and disappear from the face of the earth." Viola vents angrily, "Oh God, I can't cope with it anymore. What a hurrah's nest it is in here! What chokes you more than the dirt and the dust bunny in this house is the disorder. Chewing gum stuck on picture frames. Drink cans thrown behind the couch and armchairs. Dishes placed in the washing machine. This is enough! Even the kingdom of chaos would disintegrate into this crumbling mess, like a piece of sponge in a bucket of acid, while you have time to complain to me about a sting."

"Well, great things begin with a sting, my dear Viola." I answer calmly as a millpond, "Here, for example, the scientists think that the entire universe was created by the bite of an atom on itself."

"Of course, dear boy, absolutely." Viola exclaims, waving her right hand above with disdain, "If it is as you say, then it means that I have created some sort of a universe every time I get sweaty, and I have pinched and scratched my rear during work."

"You may never know." I answer and let out a belly laugh, "A universe or an abyss that swallows and snuffs the light out even of the brightest star; you might have created this, considering all your unsaturated body fat. And who knows what the instant has in store for one?! Besides, after all, you have agreed of your own free will to work here. No one forced you."

"Have I agreed with my free will?! Hahaha, what a divine joke!" Viola guffaws, "I don't know how free I am when the hungry eyes of my little one clasp me as if in a trap when I return home after work." she tells me in a serious tone of voice, "Or when the icy gaze of my employer sees in me human capital for gaining profits, which must stand next to a machine, and not only that but resemble it and adapt to it as much as possible. This is my experience in a shoe factory, where I have to work during the mornings. I have to complete a minimum of five hundred and sixty tasks throughout the day, including visiting the bathroom twice, to produce twenty units of goods. And when it comes to the salary, it is so high that you will never be able to emerge from the jaws of destitution. That is, in my case, enough to keep me languishing. Ah...! That's not free will, darling, except if by free will you consider necessity and opportunism that takes hold of your head, as if by pincers. But what can one do?! Necessary evil!"

"I would have preferred that we paid you more because of the great job you do here, but we only have so many options." I answer, not knowing what to add further.

"But no, sweetheart, I didn't mean that. I was just venting the anger accumulating in my chest all these years. Besides, the twice a week and for two hours a day that I come and work in this house, even if you didn't pay me anything, I would do it voluntarily." says Viola with a sad voice, "The truth is, I have not seen slime in such proportions anywhere else, but I still like working here because I feel that all my talents are emphasised and appreciated. Of course, moral evaluation is dearer to me than any monetary gain. Although it is a bit difficult to make a clear differentiation between them, as they interact closely. The thing is, I like to clean. Everything I touch, I scour it out and make it shine like a diamond before it goes to the auction, and the deeper the diamond is dug from the earth, the brighter it shines. The same goes for your house. What's more, there are no sneaky eyes here to keep watch over you around the clock, and at the end of the day, even though I may be exhausted and physically crushed by fatigue, I feel light-hearted and spiritually exhilarated." Viola concludes with a very melodious and happy voice.

"In that case, you always have a handshake from me, which pulsates with thanks and gratitude. The relaxing moments we spend in this house, welcoming us all spruced up thanks to your care, is a feeling money can't buy." I tell her kindly and reach out to shake her hand.

"Hehehe... Now you pissed me off!" Viola scolds me and withdraws her hand without touching mine, "I, dear boy, so you may know, I have worked humbly everywhere, as busy as a bee. I have gone through many trials in my life, and experience calls me to draw your attention to a few things."

I realize that Viola is in the mood for a shoulder to cry on but also to feel useful by giving advice. I am always all ears about what she had to say, but this time, I was on edge to meet Ikun right away, and I wanted to break away as soon as possible to meet her.

"I know, Viola, how hardworking you are. It is enough for me just to look around, and your name is signed within the comfort that invites me to rest in this house. Save some of your advice for next time because I have to go upstairs and meet Ikun. It's been a while since I have seen her, and lately, we can't even get to greet each other as we should."

"Is it Ikun you are looking for? It's only been a short time since she popped off for a shower. Go on, sit on the sofa by the hearth and, although the fire is not lit, I will try to warm the atmosphere a little with my stories." Viola tells me, and thus stoops down to pick up the mop that had fallen on the floor, "Go sit down, I'll give the corridor a final touch, and I'm done."

In the living room, stands an old ocher oval beech table by the window and seven chairs engraved by frequent repairs over the years. Opposite it is the couch draped in light brown calico, embroidered with flora and bird patterns, flanked by two armchairs. Yet what draws the eye as soon as you walk in is the huge mantelpiece built into the wall between the sofa and the door. Spanning over a meter in length and nearly two in width, it resembles a prehistoric cave that hides fossils of past civilizations and where, during the winter, through the irreplaceable moments we spend in each other's company, tales and stories are set ablaze as if in a crematorium. Meanwhile, after putting her final touches to the corridor, Viola comes and sits next to me, starting to speak thus "Ehhh, dear T.! So that you know, my hardship started before I ever took my first breath. Back then, when the war was just over, my family found itself in a rather peculiar position. My lineage is quite extensive, with many branches and cousins up to seven generations, most of whom I neither know nor have had any contact with. Kinfolks of mine were involved as quislings and collaborators with foreign powers in the administration of the city during the occupation. Nonetheless, our relatives took up arms and joined the liberation forces, fighting against the invaders and their supporters by self-sacrificing and cowering down only to conscience. One such man was the son of my father's aunt, who was martyred for the fatherland during the conflict. We were a quiet family of petty traders who did not involve ourselves with politics. After the war, due to some unfavourable circumstances and overzealousness in the craft of espionage, my family and I were classified as traitors.

The blood that flowed from our veins was as tainted as the one that flowed in the veins of *Kaio Shpargu*, a certain major, a second cousin of my father, who had carried out bloody military actions against the liberation forces. In truth, the wounded from both warring sides were sheltered in our house, of course, at different times. During the war, it was the liberation forces, and at the end of it, the occupying troops, who had just capitulated. This is because we had a holy law at home, in which the needy being who knocked on our door was not given the cold shoulder, and the bun from the hearth was divided among all, with a little bit of salt and a glad heart. But it happens that the heart in the pan often becomes a feast for the wicked and the base. This is exactly what did occur to us one day while we were sheltering some ex-soldiers of the occupying forces who had already surrendered, with the rest fleeing wherever they could after their battalion collapsed. Then, the Neighbourhood's Plenipotentiary came to visit our house.

He was a kind of provocateur of the regime, its sensory tentacle in a way, triggered to act blindly in pulling the rug under the feet of those suspected of being opponents and crooks of the commonwealth of the people. While the Plenipotentiary was thanking my father for the support we had given to the liberation forces during the war, he noticed some bandages covered in blood at the corner of the wall, near the sofa, in the waiting room. After he left the house, the military police stormed in, and they found the wounded soldiers in the basement. All these events I have pictured in my imagination as vivid illustrations from the stories my father used to narrate to me when he came in the evening from work and tucked me in bed so that I could fall asleep." Viola stammers the last words.

"And so, in the blink of an eye," she continues with somewhat shortness of breath, "our family was branded as kulaks, quislings, bloodsuckers of the working masses, and I don't know what else. As the saying goes, worse than being blind is falling into disgrace. A part of our lineage, who had joined the liberation forces, cursed and disowned us. The building, the two-story ground floor house where we lived, was seized from us and nationalized for the pressing needs of the working class to put a roof over their heads. And as punishment, my family was forced to live in a faraway rural place. Several sheds, which had previously been stables for cattle, served as a roof over our heads. Like us, many other families were exiled to live in that area. When this happened, my family consisted of four members: my mother, my father, my paternal grandmother, and my older brother, who was then only one year old. I was born in the same camp a few years later. We were forced to cook in the toilet in that shelter, as the room was like a sardine box. Two donkey breakfast bunks were fixed to one side of the wall as in a submarine, and there was no room to swing a cat. On the opposite side, a small portable table was also mounted, which, when laid down, fell beside the bed and blocked that little narrow strip of the corridor from the door to the bathroom. When I was born, since there was no more space to add another bed in that kennel room, in the uno thread where the lamp is screwed, we hung a cradle with a thick coated cable in which I slept. In the morning, we took it off again so as not to hinder the passage. We repeated this ritual until I was three years old. After my grandmother passed away, that dear and gentle soul, I took her bed." In the last sentence, Viola's voice faded almost to a whisper, and her eyes darted rapidly.

"Uff..., what else can I tell you about our countless hardships we endured," she resumes as if awakened, reinvigorated from a lethargic sleep, "The door to our bathroom was made from old linen, worn and thin as cigarette paper, for the front door, we adapted what had once been the portico of an abandoned pantry. For the function of the window, the only one we had in the room, through which the first rays of the dawn flowed in, we had fashioned a plastic sheet nailed to some wooden slats. I remember how the light that poured through it into the room was always dim and nebulous, like a gloomy winter's day, because of the plastic sheets, which, although translucent, were still not as clear as glass. And glass, back then, was in short supply, like scarce water in a desert, and was not at hand for everyone. We changed the plastic covering as often as we could, as it scorched and melted because of exposure to frequent temperature changes. My father managed to secure the plastic films in the town's workshop, where he worked as a roustabout, even though he was a graduate in economics. Sometimes, when transparent plastic coverings were not in stock, my father had to bring in coloured sheets. You can't imagine how happy I felt when the windows glittered bright yellow, sometimes green, red or blue, refracting their light on all four corners of the room. I felt like I was somewhere else, in a world of fairy tales and myths. For a long time, the colours in that room and the seasons were the only things that experienced any transition. Although in rags and abhorrently wronged, we were nurtured not to harbour any hatred towards those who brought lumps to us on a day-to-day basis because, as my father used to say, they were not free to think for themselves. On the contrary, in pitifulness, we saw how, day by day, madness crept over their heads and made those people vegetate in irrationality. For many of those who persecuted us, it had become necessary to target someone as the enemy so that even if there were no more enemies to target, they would be created with wickedness and then brought down with a lot of populism, allegedly by the will of the people. Everything was arranged to run like clockwork."

"It's only been a few days since I met someone I have known since I was a kid, and he underwent an ordeal when the country was in the throes of regime collapse." I intervene, confused and fascinated by Viola's story, as well as by her captivating narration style, "His story has haunted me all these days; it was so creepy. But please, continue." I address her full of wonder, like a small child.

"Where was I? Ah, aj..." she gathers her wits. And, like a caring granny, she carries on with her storytelling, "I love learning so much and graduated from high school with high scores. I really wanted to complete my advanced studies in history and geography because I always wondered and longed for the world behind the barbed wire-stuffed borders. But this was almost impossible for many, even more so for a girl my age. And how could the enemies of

128

the people be allowed to benefit from public education so carefully cultivated by the nomenclature? We were seen simply as snails seeking to drool over the mushroom of knowledge that rose day by day with the spirit of the one-party state. To be honest, even if the families had no blot on their escutcheon, not all of their children were allowed to attend higher university courses because there was a deficit in training the population for various skills and professional trades. In the end, I was assigned to start work in an agricultural cooperative near the town where I lived. I did not regret this decision because my love for animals and nature was great and grew stronger each day. As my father used to tell me, in these last hundred years, there had been more murder, destruction and chaos planted by the hand of man on this earth than by nature in thousands of years." Viola's voice brightens as she concludes, and an almost poisonous smile begins to curl at the edge of her lips.

"Though never before have we experienced in a few decades as much development as then!" I add as Viola is about to finish her sentence.

"What do you mean by this, that progress comes through violence, and thanks to war and destruction?!" Viola jumps in as if suddenly being bitten by a snake, "Ah, you troublemaker, who plays cat and mouse with the shadows of my past." she adds, and her face starts to glow up, "As far as I have understood, I can say that war is a race after an ideal that we posit in this world at a certain time. Where everyone runs after their own polar star and, like little children running in a misty field filled with lightning bugs, bump into each other. A dirty but inevitable fog is the pervasive misunderstanding. Worse still are one-sided, malicious interpretations. Here, for example, during the time I worked in the cooperative, several 'reforms' took place, such as the herding of cattle, where the villagers were stripped of the right to rear even a single chicken or to plant a crop of tomatoes in their backyards. All livestock then would be bred in cooperatives in the name of the people and the one-party state that governed. It was an awkward situation, where in the villages, the only cock in the henhouse that could be heard singing at dawn on the rooftops were the censored news programs on radio and television. Then it was also sought that the bellows of cows and baa of sheep and goats were to praise the centralized economy. The peasant was no longer a peasant but a serf who worked for wages, no longer for the local landlord but for the central government. Without his free thought, the citizen was no longer a citizen but a lifeless cog in the state machinery. So, one of the most painful things I had to witness at that time was the shedding of the qualities that make a person a human being."

"Now that you are telling me this story, I am thinking of what my old pal told me, and you are absolutely right." I reinforce her last sentence, "No one should be treated inhumanely because, on the one hand, the one who is mistreated gives up hope for the future, while the one who illtreats destroys his hope by biting his nose off and spitting on his face."

"That's right, except that the popular expression 'if he beats you, it means he loves you' is still in circulation." Viola vents, not without irritation, "This expression has always seemed to me to be a hoax because, according to this expression, it is appropriate for you to embrace violence in order to destroy the humanity of someone you love. But never mind, different strokes for different folks… as I was saying, it was the state machine itself that subdued the individual values. Everyone has the opportunity to develop and process those according to their own will in a dynamic social environment. But a virtuous individual can agree to sacrifice himself for a major cause, such as the homeland, or society and family. He can even put himself under the yoke of the state machine to achieve goals and protect certain values, but only if this is done with his free choice. It is impossible to force such an individual against his will because he views opportunism with contempt and necessity as a condition to be overcome.

In this way, virtuous individuals with opposing political views were oppressed as enemies of the people and reactionaries because they were also among the most bound and determined. There was no longer a need for original ideas and personal initiatives. The value templates were waxed and ready for everyone to adopt. You just had to absorb them, like a sponge soaking up water.

Individuals in society were treated like eagles, who were nursed to old age and never taught how to fly. Every time I remember my generation, I regret that from the beginning, they were buried under their own faeces without being able to walk upright on their own two feet.

And as for the new generation, the future appears just as bleak. The reins of power, once gripped by 'tyranny', are now manipulated by corruption. At least before, 'the Tyrant' had an end in sight, however close or far in time it may be. Whereas now, we have to dance for eternity under the illusion that we are all responsible and no one is guilty.

I can't forget how the primary school teacher wrinkled her lips, squeezed and squirmed when she received a modest bunch of flowers from my daughter on Teacher's Day. 'Dear God, I thought, in what kind of hell am I raising my children!' I thought. Shouldn't a holiday called 'Without Bribery Day' be added to the calendar?

All these years, I have dreamed that the People's Parliament was made up of all the individual members of that society to which it belongs." Viola fires off as if she is reading a holographic will, with her eyes directed upwards and with a peaceful smile on her face, "A society where the right of representation doesn't need to be delegated to someone else. And with today's technology, it is possible for all people to participate in discussions about the common future, where they are a factor.

A society where judges impose their rulings on themselves first before they become binding on anyone else.

Where the investigators do not inspect matters of the heart, because, if they did, their own bloody words would find themselves there.

Where the cops don't ride the bull of the state wagon backwards, and then complain about society regressing.

Where doctors, teachers and educators, and the institutions where they work, are the workshops where the hardworking and virtuous citizen enjoys the mushroom of knowledge, and not labyrinths where they are tricked by the wicked and the bone-idle...

In a word, the system, or social contract that the members of a society make with each other, does not compel some to prostitute their abilities to satisfy the whims and the lusts of others. But where the social contract should inspire one to carry out their duty with conviction and diligence, regardless of the circumstances. So, a society where everyone feels self-sufficient, without the need to use elbows to get somewhere, because the success of the other will belong to him, and the other way around.

Sleep, sonny, close your eyes, because only the next generation can reap the fruits of our dreams!

We just prepare the ground so the seed might grow..." these are the last of Viola's words I am able to hear, because when the couch and I meet, sleep is just around the corner.

*   *   *

Not even five minutes had passed, which seemed like an eternity to me, when little by little, the superficial layer of calmness that had gripped my being start to dissolve. Drowsy, while blinking my eyelids, I thought I was in a cave. From the many stalactites scattered around its dome, water droplets are dripping and soaking my face.

As I sober up and my vision clears, the stalactites and the view I had imagined only a few moments ago shifts in a flash, and Ikun's hair begin to become visible as she flips her head down and squishing it over me, along with the vastness of the night, in an effort to wake me up. She stands as a divinity twirling her hair by the shore of the lake, from whose conic tips the very juice of life seems to concentrate and then drip.

Swaying back and forth, Viola had just finished work and is about to walk out the door, when I hear her say to Ikun how I had seemed tired, and as if the conversation that we were holding had suddenly been charged with numbing vapours, I had dropped off.

"The lads of our age fall asleep while standing," says Ikun.

"Yes, yes, like the horses." Viola answers, smiling, "But when lightning flashes on the horizon before the storm, and the north wind tosses their manes, those who do not gallop turn into statues."

"Indeed! They turn into hard granite rocks, my dear Viola, as if the Fairies had wasted them away. But this flying unicorn that lies here flinches even when lightning cracks across a clear blue sky, let alone when the dark clouds gather menacingly around him."

"Precisely, how did you come up with that?!" Viola says, bursting out laughing as she crosses the threshold of the door.

Ikun had not long been back home from work. Still dozy, juggling words in the air with her, I learn that Behar had been having health complications, so he would have to remain under the strict care of the white coats for a few more days. As she was getting ready to visit him in the hospital, she asks whether I might accompany her. I let her know that I was completely at her disposal that evening, and we promptly hit the road.

The mist has thickened somewhat, and the morning clouds up high in the sky scrumptiously accompany us in every step we take. The full moon bathes the milky light like a beacon through the clouds, licking and shining Ikun's face, neck and bare limbs. Dressed in a dark blue backless dress of silk, the folds of which outline her curves and match up in space with the winding lines of the mountainous range to the east of the city, one may discern from afar the whole of her body that shines like some star fluttering down from the farthest ends of the universe. Tonight, Ikun's every movement and facial expression radiates an extraordinary alluring charm. When I ask her why she was dressed up so swish, she replies that she did so because of the respect and gratitude she has for the hospital environment, the place where, with its gasps, death seeks to extinguish the warm flame of the candle of life. For Ikun, that institution symbolizes a gate through which the soul is transported to the other world. And if once a week you had to dress up smart to go to the church, mosque, theatre or opera, places from which everyday trifles are seen from different angles, and that in particular echo the "moment" when the soul breaks away from tragedies and earthly pains, then there was no reason why she should not do the same, and dress glamorously on this occasion as well.

"After all, in the hospital, it is not necessary to pretend or stimulate the imagination of the 'last moment' with all kinds of extravagances. Everything there is so real and straightforward." Ikun stresses.

And I couldn't agree more with her on many points. But nevertheless, I held the opinion that looking at the hospital superficially from the outside, we necessarily saw it clothed in a veil of mysticism, superstition and prejudice. Also, I was convinced that the internal staff saw the picture from a different point of view. That a physician saw the dysfunction of one organ or the injury of another as a cobbler sees with the eyes nearly popping out of his head the torn boots of a bum; certainly with the thought and desire to fix the anomaly and to bring it back to the ordinary course of things. Where "the ordinary" means the healthy and uninterrupted state of performing the function for this organ before the injury. So, after a while, the means and methods of healing a sick patient, which at first seem surprising and mystical, turn into routine and mechanical actions predetermined to the details. A job like any other, where the doctor hopes that after the treatment, the organ will again be able to support the flow of life like the shoemaker hopes that the repaired shoe will adequately wrap the sole of the foot to protect it from external environmental agents and to facilitate walking and moving as cosy as possible. In both cases, nothing was one hundred per cent certain, as many factors must interact appropriately and, thankfully, not in a singular harmony. Everything depends on the main factor, on life itself. Would it accept, or not, this rearranged matter as an auxiliary instrument in its continual and unceasing manifestation and regeneration? This is the junction where the calculation of possibilities and what lies beyond it begins. This is where hope and faith have their genesis.

While we were discussing all this, drops of rain, increasing in intensity, start to fall, first moistening our heads and then our shoulders. I take off the jacket I am wearing and throw it over her fragile shoulders. Around us, the umbrellas unfurl one after the other popping open like parachutes during a military freefall, while the toddling along by the many passers-by who frequent the streets in the city centre, through which we have to pass to get to the hospital, becomes more frequent and more distorted. Drivers steer their cars more slowly than usual due to the wet roads steeped in fog. Spits and spots of rain continue to fall, and due to the illumination projected by the headlights of the never-ending procession of vehicles that glide past us, a pale shimmering halo is created around our bodies. Facing the concatenation of cars, for a moment, one gets the impression that a multitude of twinkling lights, like bright, sleepy jellyfish, wander on the road without direction or compass. A kind of inexplicable joy and wonder seizes us. While we are talking, I could not take my eyes off the nape of her neck, which in those moments resembled a mountain pass, where the freshly fallen and red and yellow autumn leaves cover with oblivion every inch. Finally, as if to completely invalidate my arguments up to that point,

Ikun tells me that although the words I use were beautiful and gracefully chosen, she still could not take them for real, as they were lifeless, like the dishevelled fur of a marten. Even though the fur shines more than in its natural state, it is fake, like this jacket I had thrown over her shoulders, which was not even mine. Her assessment was really harsh and caught me off guard, so I thought to twist it into a pun, and told her that even the marten itself could not have dreamed of a better afterlife for its fur than to shine on its victims after it had died. After all, there is nothing else like your skin! But better be a conscientious deceiver than a bait for misunderstandings and social-hysteria. She returns my last remark with a sneer and adds that sometimes I seemed so ridiculous that, truly, she didn't know what to make of me. I was either quite innocent, like a child's heart, or a shadow that slinked around other people's words and arguments.

But for me, the matter was quite different. I was aware that I could not define even the slightest thing in the world without using the words and arguments that society, in general, used up to that time as instruments. And I would be truly happy and a genius, if only once in my life I could create a new word out of nothing. I merely picked and chose between words or expressions that I heard here and there that, at the end of the day, boiled down in my mind and then tried to transform or use them from a different perspective. So, for example, I told her what had happened a few days ago in a fruit and vegetable market, where I had accidentally caught a snippet of the conversation while walking by "... you must be quite gooey to do that...", which I used the next day twisting it in a conversation with some friends of mine, facetiously telling one of them how he must be quite ghouly to do that, something he had already performed that day. At most, I could summarize various phenomena and events in an archaic word that was no longer used, thus giving it a fresh, secondary meaning, different from the first one. But if only I could create a new word?! This was impossible for me but only a challenge to poets and prophets, whose spiritual reverberations thunder more than the menacing lightning bolts of the Olympian god. A spiritual resonance in which unselfishness and impotence alienate them towards oneness. An inner calling that, in a contradictory way, demanded the disintegration and annihilation of the self towards oneness with the eternal. A march towards absolute alienation. On the other hand, I tried to convince Ikun that I was just a "Comanche", and in every confrontation I had over the years, whether those against an individual or society taken as a whole, the only thing I had gained were words and expressions of others, as the only trophies of my achievements.

Blithe as we were, the conversation flows freely, so much so that sometimes it sounds to me that words and sentences waltz around to the rhythm of the timeless. In particular, they resonate on her lips and with a shudder, cleared the road ahead and spread out, caressing the asphalt, sidewalks and walls of the buildings around. Lastly, I confided to her that since I had worn her fiancé's jacket, I hadn't felt alone anymore.

By then, we arrive in front of the hospital entrance. The multi-story, long, L-shaped building echoes with perplexing voices. The lobby and hallways glow with a dim and pallid neon light that seems to disinfect everything in and around the building with chlorine. At the same time, a feeling of dirt and filthiness, hidden behind the density of the whiteness thrown by the neon lights, gets into you. A filth whose origin cannot be pinpointed, and as a result, anxiety clings to your chest and torments you nonstop.

Family members swarming from all directions are escorting their relatives in large numbers as if they are leading them to a procession in front of an altar to celebrate the love for life, be it sacrificial.

The medical-surgical patient room where Behar is recuperating is not far from the entrance. We found him bedridden with his eyes closed, breathing with difficulty through two plastic tubes connected to the gurgling oxygen machine. About six people are lying down one after the other in the room, all without exception, connected by multiple threads to life-support devices with flashing lights and notifications on their screens. For a moment, due to the noises that the machines emit, mixed with occasional sighs and groans from the patients, the impression is created that a non-human creature resides and interacts with the sick. Although half-conscious, Behar has spotted us and, with dry lips aching smiles at us with sparkling eyes.

"Welcome to my alpine transhumance!" he stammers and then tries to stand up, but in vain, his powers betray him, and shuddering, he tumbles back into the bed.

"Do not push yourself, Behar," intervenes Ikun, " because you are still feeble. We have brought you fresh fruit juices to soothe your throat and help you recover."

"What good are those to me, my lass?! Ah, what clean air! Can you hear how the water of the spring glugs?" which in reality, were the gurgling sounds from the oxygen machine, "Only that and the sunlight can bring me to my senses. Ah, sunlight! Where are you? Rock me once again in your arms, like you used to do when I was a child. What are these greyish clouds weighing down on my eyelids?!"

"Not two days have passed since you had a liver operation," answers Ikun, "Apparently, the blessed organ distilled the last sip of brandy, because you can't drink even a drop anymore after what you've been through."

"What are you telling me? Booze, my mistress of so many marinated times, will visit me no longer? And what will I do now in the dark, empty nights, when my eye wanders the deserted alleys, and my gullet dries up, and I won't be able to wet my whistle? Like gall, from now on, my days will leak grief, and they will freeze one by one upon the edge of my lip."

"Calm down, Behar," I try to comfort him, "because you still haven't fully recovered yet. You're lucky to still be alive."

"Eh, my good lad! Do you call *buona fortuna* this crippled life that I have left after that horrible news that you just gave me?! Now, when the sun drops from the horizon, I have to wear a straitjacket so that I don't disintegrate like some shadow of a goblin in the density of the twilight. The second option is to get lost in some desert, in the middle of nowhere, and pull the trigger on myself there. And let the blood from the knocked-over cup be swallowed by the Mother Earth and cleanse it, and then let new life arise. Was it not enough for this vale of tears, at the height of its blood gluttony, to bite my liver, but now it wants me to give my last breath by vegetating when, in fact, it has sucked my thirsty soul out of my body from this very day."

"What do you mean?" Ikun jumps in with a face as long as a fiddle, "you can't lose hope and give up."

"Eh, dearest missy! If there was anything that could keep me attached to this life, it is your pure and sweet smile, like the scent of roses, and the kindness of both of you who opened your hearts and turned them into a warm nest for me. But I don't deserve it. I am nothing but a skid-row bum, for where I rise in the morning, I do not fall at night. An endless struggle to escape from myself since I lost my lord. Those events still hang over me like a black cloud, and all the feelings and emotions seem to evaporate out of my body, leaving me utterly desolate. Since then, only that joy juice could sweeten the bitter hours of my days."

As soon as he pronounces the last word, he coughs a few times, fixes the oxygen tubes, and propped himself up on his elbows. Then he leans his back on the side of the bed. His pale face is brightening up by a shadow of a smile. Ikun and I, from time to time, look into each other's eyes, and then our gazes focus entirely on Behar. Thus, there were pauses, moments which served him to compose himself and spin from the tangle of his thoughts, which in those moments were badly intermingled.

"The road has not always been a home for me, nor has tippler been my profession." Behar begins to speak, "This mangy goat you see here was part of an elite troop carefully selected to secure the lives of the leaders of the previous regime."

"What?! You were part of the governmental agency of the Secret Services?!" Ikun cries out, aghast at his confession.

"Yes, that's how it is. Among other things, I, like many others, also served as a channel of communication between the top of the pyramid of power and the people. During the day, we, along with other closest associates, circled about our leaders like the earth around the sun. When we spent time with them, we carried mirrors so big that we could barely hold them with both hands wide open while we kept our heads crouched behind the polished glass. They would go stark raving bonkers with joy when their conversation with us sparked any idea of how to gather more might into their hands. It was assumed that the thinking behind it was the fruit of the conversation with their image, which excited them to the point of becoming drunk with power. However, the thought that the space where their being resides is immeasurable, an illusion created by countless mirrors reflecting at one another, gave them complacency and the peace of mind to make them more rapacious creatures. When any of us inadvertently communicated directly with them, not having the mirror in between, they'd become unhinged and turned into monsters. And you had to be something of a beast yourself so that their bite wouldn't be mortal."

After a short pause, he adds, "During the night, we merged into one with the people."

Saying that Behar hushed down and a wall of silence rose between us. But this time, the eloquent silence shouts in our minds questions of the most different kind. Who is Behar in reality? Was our encounter pure coincidence, or was it planned on purpose? Just the thought that he had been part of that tangled web, which he just told us, made us quake in our boots and swallow back into the pit of our stomach every whisper of the voice that strained to pass and come to the surface in the form of a word or a reaction. What was his role in that enigmatic structure, which is still a mystery to this day? Finally, Ikun broke the silence and addressed him thoughtfully "Why didn't you tell us about this before, Behar?"

"Well, how should I put it?" he said, he says, muttering to himself, and after a short halt, carries on "When you found me that morning in those bushes, I was in my original environment. A savage out in the wild. The next morning, when I woke up at your house, I felt like I was a child again, and I was in my room, where I was born and grew up. I wanted that feeling to last as long as it could, and when you offered me a place to stay, it was impossible for me not to accept it. I was afraid that if I told you my story, you wouldn't let me come and darken your doorstep. That is why."

"Blimey, our house is bathed in crocodile tears?" I made a remark that I almost regretted.

"Your guess is not far from the truth, Behar." Ikun picks up the conversation again, "And there is no way it could be otherwise if you take into account all the horrible deeds that we have heard and are propagating about the agency where you were once employed. From childhood, we were accustomed to the tales told to us by adults about the herd that was threatened by the wolf, which, in its state of fury, drowns more victims than it can feed on. That's why society is organized in such a way; it develops structures to protect itself from such a beastly impulse. But for one to turn itself into a predator?! This is obviously a contradiction to the original mission of the organisation, which I am not able to understand at all."

In the meantime, Behar becomes short-winded, and a raspy hiss begins to scratch his throat with every breath he takes. His eyeballs dilate slightly, and his eyelids hang motionless for a few moments. At last, after rubbing his upper lip with his first two teeth as usual and coughing several times to clear his throat, he begins to speak "Eh, my dear lassie! How beautiful it would be if, as in the fairy tales, good triumphs over evil in the end. Or, in this case, as if some sheep smothered the wolf with kisses! But can such a thing happen?! No, not at all. Evil can only be annihilated. And every annihilation, whatever it may be, contains elements of evil, such as violence, tension, dissolution. So, our structure was developed to eliminate this base instinct. And the only way to do that was for this structure to turn into another kind of monster, which cold-bloodedly targets a single individual as the personification of evil to horrify and then devour him. It was this necessary evil that would henceforth keep the herd safe."

"How can an organism that has streams of blood for its diet be justified in this way?" Ikun says, at her wits' end, "And, please, the mathematical trick that, in difficult moments, you can exchange one life to save a hundred others won't help justify yourself much. This logic is not valid. After all, rivers form from the merging of streams. Basically, they are the same."

"Ah, my sweet young thing, if only things, in general, were that simple." says Behar, slightly sticking out his tongue to lick his chapped lips, "In our profession, discipline is a primary virtue that does not need to be preached. The days of service, at that time, came and went unbendingly as if they were tin leaves of an iron book. Our agency was a lancet operating on the body of society. Just as in ancient times, vein cutting was practiced to treat a variety of diseases; in the same way, we acted on society, given that we were doing the best with the tools and knowledge we had up to that time. Same as anyone else in our place would have done."

"Don't say that." Ikun interrupts him, "I'd never harm a soul if, at least, they would not give me back a smile of gratitude."

"Nor would I, gorgeous, do something if I didn't get a smile of gratitude for my services." Behar turns to her with a smile, "I must add that I wouldn't even lift a finger if I didn't take the smile as an advance. An old professional knack, which was mandatory for the job position we were covering. It was the smile of the 'Leader' that was reflected

144

in our lancet, while we were a reflection of society in his mind. He was the one who defined the diagnosis, while we acted imbued with the good intention to make the sick patient healthy again."

At this point, Ikun seems resigned and stunned by the things she was hearing from Behar's mouth. She is at the same time confused and disappointed. A hunch urges me that I have to take hold of the reins of the conversation if I don't want her to give up the ghost at this point. So, I hastily address Behar "Do you think you are healthier than you were? You look like death eating a cracker. Take a look around. Just as I was coming to you, the faces of some castor oil artists with gamblers' countenances bumped into me in the corridor. As I entered the room, I had to shoo off a couple of nurses who moved around you like vultures circling a carcass."

"Ha, ha, ha! You really creasing me up, boy." Behar grinned and bore it, while holding his belly with his hands because of the pain, "You satisfied my craving for the past. Isn't it like a three-ring circus in here? Day after day, a crowd of doctors, led by their professor, flocks from unit to unit, making their rounds and carefully watching the progress of the patients through the charts. The professor in charge of them, a gaunt man, about one head shorter than me, with bright and lustrous eyes like those of a shrew-mole, slabhead, with wrinkles that start just above the eyebrows and end behind the back of his head, waves to the crowd of apprentice doctors and from there, a bigboned man with narrow shoulders, and a low bass voice approaches hunching over him and whispers something in his ear. I believe that he tells him about the test results or something similar to a preliminary diagnosis. Meanwhile, the professor does not utter a sound but listens thoughtfully, cocking an eye at the patient. And as soon as the big-boned man finishes what he has to say, the professor approaches the patient, strips him from the waist above, and then, with sharp moves, pinches the abdomen around the aching area as if he is looking to examine the wound under the skin with the tip of the fingers. His dexterous actions are closer to a martial arts master than to a petty authority. Meanwhile, the crowd of doctors chasing after him, all of whom, without exception, are equipped with old cameras with retro flashes, snap one photo after another so as not to miss a single movement of my reactions. Then the professor makes recommendations for further treatment, and the whole lot thunder across to the adjacent bed to examine the next case.

Ah, the sparks flashing from all four sides, and we both performing the dance of life and death... Where are you, my lord? Why did you abandon me... Ah, drink, the cruel mistress of my soul!..."

After these broken phrases, Behar falls back into unconsciousness, and the rest of the words he utters in delirium are incomprehensible to our ears. His sobs join the chorus of the other moaning patients in the room, whereas the alarm sounds of several nearby medical equipment draw the attention of the nurses, who rush into the room to settle the situation.

At this time, Ikun pulls me by the sleeve and signals me to leave, so we can give Behar a chance to gather his strength. Outside, the rain has stopped, but the washed streets, still-dripping trees, and everything else are glistering, like the surface of a lake, when the moon and the stars are reflected. The night is liquefied and mysteriously lurking everywhere. The conversation with Behar had left deep impressions on us, which is clearly visible from our

146

flashing faces. As soon as one of us attempts to strike up a conversation, the words fail us, having uttered only the first syllable. We are in a tizzle, and our hearts are thumping like little sparrows that the thunderstorm had taken by surprise and forced to cower down under the shelter of an abandoned building. My mind is made up that even if Behar had been the hobgoblin, it was impossible to set to naught the bread we had broken between us. Even more so when he had made a clean breast of everything. And if we were to drum him out of the house now, it would be as if we had left him buried under the layer of frost that morning where we first found him.

As for Ikun, I had no doubt that she had already forgiven him for not confessing and keeping his past a hidden. Her conscience could not bear to keep a grudge above the surface, and everything weighty and improper sank deep once and for all. Anyway, we didn't say a word until we got home. She had lost none of her former glow of that night; on the contrary, our visit to the hospital had put her under pressure, and thus, she radiates even more kindness from her inner world.

She sways sweetly side to side around the house, as the tongue-like shapes of a beacon or a candle, as a light breeze blew from outside. It is only after we part and go to our rooms that the dizziness appeased and the fever grips us violently with chills and thrills.

*   *   *

The spring season this year was barely discernible. The summer brought hot weather as rarely before, and then it withdrew like a burning straw, leaving the heat behind.

Although it is the end of September, the sun vomits forth torrents of scorching air above the ground. Thus, the migration of krill, flamingos, herons, and various types of geese and ducks has been postponed by at least a few days, if not weeks. Their abode in a lagoon not far from the city, a place which I visit whenever I get the chance, buzzes all the time with various birds chirping, each adding its own unique ping. Their elegant movements—rightly described as a kind of water ballet—their remarkable agility in hunting, which would stir envy in any seasoned angler, the rhythmic beating of their wings before takeoff, and their harmonious coexistence with other species have always filled me with a sense of wonder. That lagoon is a natural resource of tranquillity and inspiration. Not much further away from this view, you find the city, gushing with the vitality and the hopes that comfortable vacations bestow on one. Kindergartens and schools, bursting at the seams with children and pupils, reverberate because of their cheerful cheers and games.

Behar, remarkably, had shaken off his illness, and you could honestly say that his appearance had been rejuvenated, at least by a few years. The summer had been quite sweltering for him, too, considering the serious ailment he had just experienced. And here I am not talking about the problems with the liver, but about his decades-long addiction to alcohol. The infernal hooch had not managed to erode all the wrinkles of his brain and thus fry his mind irrevocably. A stream of light had kept itself aloof inside him, which, by kindling the fire in his belly, brought back to his mind the unwavering military will. He had already found a part-time job as a newsagent at a kiosk near the train station and was contributing as much as he could to the house rent and everything else, even though neither Ikun nor I had urged him to do such a thing. Years ago, he had noticed a gipsy chap who disobeyed his father's order to beg on the street and, because of this, had run away from his home, a makeshift shack in the slums by the river. When it came to this chap's family members, all of whom he was not able to count on his fingers since he had more than you could shake a stick at, he simply knew that his mother kept her stork busy, experiencing one pregnancy to another without ever being able to regain her strength completely from the puerperium period.

While the father, one of the "gaffers" who routinely came home being four sheets and slapped him, but also touched his private parts, demanded more and more money from him. Only a short time before, one of his brothers, collecting scrap metal, had died by being pierced through his body by a rusty rod when he had fallen from the slab of an abandoned building and could not survive his injuries. At that time, Behar had noticed his innocent self-awareness and took care that he did not dissolve into nothingness on the streets like sugar stirred into water. He had also taught him a few tricks on how to squeeze a stingy merchant, who preferred to bury food that was about to expire rather than sell it below cost. Then he hired him as his associate in selling newspapers. This gypsy chap is now a young man and has managed to buy what he had dreamed of since childhood with the money he had saved. A grey-motley white mare, decorated with red ribbons over her ears, pulling a cart on two wheels, which he rode to deliver newspapers to subscribers. Not long ago, the mare had given birth to a white foal with brown knobs. If I were to try to coin a definition of freedom, I would say it was the sight of that foal, unbridled, going after its mother and attempting to suckle a teat.

Behar had lost something of the sense of humour that characterized him at the time we met, as well as the delirium that the booze bestows on one in abundance. This does not mean that he no longer banters with everybody, but he does it more sparingly and, at the same time, serves it with biting irony, especially for the chap on the third floor. "Top geezer," he says to him, "don't dawdle along, and while you are young, don't look at the mantelpiece when you are poking the fire." And the chap did not utter a word but lowered his head in shame like a lily and blushed as a spoiled maid. Whereas Behar converses smoothly and with pleasure with the nanny who lives on the first floor. Children are his rock of ages, and he always chews the rag with her about how you could better take care of them and how to fit into their world as best as possible. If I didn't know him better, his fatherly shadow would make me think that, most likely, he hosts a fairy tale show or writes children's stories. It came as no surprise for us to come home and find the table laid out with all the goodies. And it was not Ikun who had done such a thing, but Behar, who, as it happened, did not lack knowledge of cooking recipes from the global cuisine.

Work at the hotel carried on as normal. The guests came and went in colonies like migratory birds on the lagoon, while from the outside, the lighted rooms made the hotel look like a pine tree decorated with passion. Meanwhile, Mrs. Bekteshi had successfully crossed the quarterly time frame without failing in her most recent initiative, which made her happy and more consistent in her striving. There was no denying that Pasqualino had been the mastermind behind her success because he had the gift of the gab with many interest groups in private meetings, convincing them to join the campaign of his recently founded party. While he was staying at the hotel and was welcoming representatives of different strata of society in the conference rooms, Mrs. Bekteshi had taken it upon herself to lead this campaign on the terrain because she was more familiar with the country and its people, and her speech resonated with the voters. Behar was also involved in this effort. He was attached to this brave initiative mainly because of her and already accompanied Mrs. Bekteshi everywhere she went. The first time she caught sight of him, her eyes wandered on his frayed blue jacket and worn-out army boots; she darted me a reproachful ray, as if to scold me about in whose hands I had trusted her safety. And, seen from that point of view, she was utterly right. He looked like a mummy's bodyguard, with the dust on his jacket turning whiter than the snow on the roof.

But Behar, bred-in-the-bone with such situations, in which silence and lingering glances speak a thousand words, approached her and, with a deft movement, took her hand in his while bringing his lips to kiss it, he said "A long journey always wearies the traveller, but it is all worth it when the water of the spring is refreshing and crystal clear." and he sealed his statement as slick as a whistle by kissing her hand, which she held hanging like a grape stalk. Madam Bekteshi brightened up instantaneously by this brief gesture like a flower in spring, answering him therewith, saying in a jolly mood, "A distant traveller is the most precious stone in a queen's crown. No one better than he can truly discern when an oasis of serenity appears on the horizon." and at this moment, one could not help but notice a condensed spiritual sparkle that lit up their faces. A warm, fuzzy feeling wrapped them both in the whirlwind of further events. From time to time, she shot him a suspicious side glance. She had a reminiscence and assumed she had seen him somewhere before, but she couldn't say for sure where. Behar didn't remember anything from his confession in the hospital, and when one day Ikun and I briefly mentioned that conversation to him, he, with a pleading face, begged us to keep it between us, as it was already done. He had slammed the door in the faces of many sad personal histories of the past once and for all. So, when Mrs. Bekteshi asked him about what he did for a living before joining the campaign because he seemed quite familiar, he answered that he had previously worked as a gardener in the largest park in the city, where the artificial lake was also located, so there was a good chance to have seen him there. But she could also have glimpsed him as a spectator in the theatre hall, when she had previously been a famous actress, because at that time, after rounding off with moonshine and having spare change left, the lukewarm theatre hall made him feel snug as a bug in a rug, where he could stretch his limbs and unburden his mind.

"Do you remember when the play 'The Harvest of Love in the Season of Dreams' was staged for the first time?" Behari asked Mrs. Bekteshi when I introduced them together.

"Of course I do, as if it were only yesterday." she answered without the slightest doubt, "It took us some time before the show went underway to keep order among the spectators. And, if it weren't for a man in shabby clothes who sprang from nowhere in the theatre hall and hypnotised everybody with two words to his whim, the show would never have begun."

"And did you hear what that shabby man said to those present in the theatre hall?" Behar asked her again.

"To be honest, for us who were behind the stage, his words sounded mere gibberish, and it was impossible to make any sense of them. At the end of the performance, a stagehand told us something about it, but I don't remember exactly because we were all so emotional about the success of the performance. But whatever words poured out of his mouth must have been nothing but honey, for after that speech, not a peep was heard, as if not a soul were there. The night, after that rough start, it grew by leaps and bounds and ended up being the brightest of my entire career as an actress."

"Indeed, the show truly set the world on fire that night, and you were its extinguished ember afterwards. And I also feel fortunate to have been the spark of that fire, as I was the rag who shushed the crowd that night." Behar said with a flicker of pride in his voice.

"That is insane?! How is that possible!? You?! It's the second time you've surprised me today. And you know,

I'm not easily knocked off my feet. But, please, tell me what you said to those present that made them stay put? How did you manage to persuade front of house when even the director of the theatre himself had failed to make them keep quiet and in one place before the opening night?"

"I had never seen such a jam-packed auditorium before in my life." Behari answered, slightly bowing his head and rubbing his forehead," There were so many people's puffs and coughing in there that a windmill could easily have been set in motion. And if you add to this the state on tenterhooks of the spectators, who began to fidget, accompanied by the chattering of the teeth and knuckle cracking, uncontrolled movements of the feet and lots of whispering, you could not help but be distracted. Even if one were a buffalo chewing cud would be agitated, let alone you, the actors who that night had so much responsibility on your shoulders. An internal impulse made me lose my temper and when one is bitten by a barn mouse, a sudden rush to the head is imminent," Behar said these words under his breath, putting the back of his left hand on the right side of his mouth, " and I stood up unconsciously, as mad as a March hare, addressing these words to the audience 'Please, dear art-loving brothers and sisters, keep calm during the performance. Let the rhythm and pulse of the events of this theatrical piece become ours. And, as if we were all inside a womb, let the actors' breathing become ours too!' That's it and nothing more." Behar wrapped up.

Mrs. Bekteshi's heart was truly flattered by joy, and shaking his hand as a sign of gratitude, she said to him "Ah, my scruffy angel! There is no way this is all a coincidence. The night that I fully spread my wings as a professional actress, you were there like the lubricant of a *clype* blowing machine. I hope you will have the same auspicious influence, where the hall this time is the most intimate interior of our motherland, and actors and spectators each one of us."

"If it were up to me, I would turn into a phoenix from the ashes of spiritual fire, eternally hovering over this city. I would raise a nest nowhere else but in your heart, to be hand in hand together in each endeavour in the future." Behar answered with a ringing voice.

"Let's hope that a glowing phoenix will rise from the ashes and dust of this city, like the lava of a volcano, and not some genie's lamp, which fulfils your wishes only after you have rubbed it." said Mrs. Bekteshi with a flare of elegance. Then she took out her lavishly carved pipe decorated with red diamonds and yellow stripes, put a cigarette in it, lit it, and then puffed on it as if it had granted her last wish before the firing squad.

When Behar asked about what made her give up acting after that glorious night, she replied that certain premonitions remain voiceless, and no matter how hard you try to define them, one cannot because it excludes vesting it with any form or meaning.

Of all the talented actors of the theatre, she, as a young girl, had warmed the cockles of Behar's heart more than anyone else. Because whenever it happened that she performed a play, it made him feel as if he was the only spectator in the hall and the whole performance was unfolding around him. Just as the gaze of Mona Lisa's portrait is devoted to each person who stands in front of her, even though at different angles, in the same way, her haunting voice conveyed to each spectator the deepest feelings individually. This was her unique trait, which she utilized very tactfully during the electoral rallies in different cities, and without a doubt, made her win the hearts and minds of the people. The warm theatrical quilt, just like the sunlight piercing through a dark cave opening, had etched in Behar's mind many lines from the theatrical pieces she had played, of which, when the appropriate occasion unfolded, he recited it passionately to her.

Meanwhile, Pasqualino, juggling ideas and concepts of the most diverse kind, through his showmanship, had managed to allure Carl and his association "Puer aeternus", and soon they became his most ardent supporters. In fact, the more Mrs. Bekteshi kept him dangling through the corridors of the hotel, the more charming he became. According to the latest rumours on the grapevine, in honour of their most recent guest, Pasqualino, who would lead their fraternal to the new heights of the "promised land" of power, Karl and his associates would make him wear around his neck, whenever he came to visit them, the loyalty beads, the ring-shaped neck ornament that decorated the chest of the chief. It was a hand-knotted cord strung with each member's canine tooth. After they had pulled it out as a sign of abstinence and conquest of their own ego, they then entrusted it to Karl, the founder and leader of the association. According to the rumours that have taken wings in the city, since the work of the fraternity is carried on in utmost secrecy and its activity was always the subject of speculation, the word went that if you happened to be invited to any of their meetings, the main thing that impressed was the uniformity, not in the outer garments, which bonded its members, but the flashing glitter of the golden dental implant when they laughed, which made them look like the crew of a pirate ship during a storm. Confabulation was combusted to the zenith when it was confidently announced that the honorary guests of this association, in order to freely interact with its other cells around the world, were required to pierce an intimate part of the body, by means of a spiral-shaped silver earring. This jewellery, which symbolized the spearhead with which the society had ended the earthly life of their saint, would serve as a passport to connect with other sister associations scattered around the globe.

"A mas honor, mas dolor."[3] declared Karl at the moment when this rite was performed on Pasqualino's body, who was horrified and turned yellow-bellied even if one pulled out a single strand of his hair, let alone when his pulp was embedded by a foreign body.

The honour of me being the first member of the party of Pasqualino and Mrs. Bekteshi did not leave Karl's thoughts, who sought to be in the centre of attention at any cost. And this was interpreted in his mind that he had to be the first supporter of the initiative of others, conscious that he himself was barren from producing any significant idea. In the political movement of Mrs. Bekteshi and Pasqualinos, he unquestioningly identified himself as the embodiment of their will, and, as the saying goes, he sought to be more "Catholic than the Pope", propagating the ideology with more persistence than the founders themselves. Every time he saw me participating in various discussions that were taking place, he whispered in Pasqualino's ear: "He is a good fellow, but 'No tener dos dedos de frente'[4] ".

Initially, the gatherings were sparse, and the people who attended them could be counted on the fingers of one hand, but very soon, those meetings turned into a sensational event, as eventually, dance parties were also organized. "After a heated conversation, and sometimes

---

[3] The more danger, the more honor.
[4] Does not have two brain cells to rub together.

158

not short of mind-boggling, I want every one of you by the end of the night shaking your tail feather so that the objectives and goals we talked about today should fall into place." Pasqualino brought his speech to an end with a quip. And it was certain that people were there to entertain themselves rather than to listen to the talks of Pasqualino and Mrs. Bekteshi. But in the end, it mattered little, for as long as the hall was thronged, and as long as the image conveyed that the political movement was supported by an army of members impregnated with merry ideals, the persons who attended these meetings might even sleep through the oration if they wished to do so.

This novel popular front has drummed up the echo spreading throughout the country. The fever of the general election campaign was beginning to set in as it rocked the city with loud and sensational news that fell on the media's parcel like fallen mulberries under the tree. Traditional politicians, their public appearances becoming more frequent with the approaching election date, targeted the ordinary citizen and put all their skills to work, fulminating the general public with all sorts of contradictory and false messages. I say, veteran politicians, as they were distinguished from the rising ones by their facial expressions. Some try to conserve the sparkle that catapulted them to power burning in their bosoms. But after a couple of mandates, their hearts had turned as black as coal, which, in addition to the heat, gave off smoke that darkened their cheeks, forming a permanent layer of scum and insolence. When they held rallies, their faces resembled a blackout cloth, where something that negated the message they were trying to convey with words swirled about. This was what betrayed them the most. That fragile sensation, which had been dragged by a thousand

and one subterranean tunnels to rumble to the surface, leading them down the political path, had dwindled away, draining its waters to the mill of vanity and stupidity. I do not know whether this is because the spring did not sprit its former waters anymore and dried up, as happens with rivers during long periods of heat, or whether their prime eruption shrivelled on the minds of the people and voters and no longer made any impression on them. But I can only say that through their body language, as they discoursed in public, a lazy muscle had been uprising without them noticing it, which refuted every word as soon as they poured it out of their mouths.

The hot weather of the summer had cut a swath through the city, pouring scorching waves, not only on the minds of the authority in power who were already legislating nothing but barren policies but also on the neighbourhood where Ilir lives. The streets leading to his house warp with countless bubbling tar, and the pavement buckles with the wall-harling groaning of fiery waves of accumulated heat. It seems as if the kingdom of the blaze has reached out everywhere with its deadly touch, devouring everything in its path, not even sparing the garden of his house. The greenery that covered the yard just a few months ago has turned into a vague mass of mixed browns with yellow colours and the occasional patches of green. The only plants that seem to have been enlivened by embracing the incendiary spirit were the bushes, brambles, and cacti, which, with the tip pointed upwards, imploringly sip from the sun every solar particle it tosses down. The once verdant thicket of roses lining the backyard wall has been condemned to the same fate. The flowers have dried up, exposing the stems, which have surprisingly thickened even more. The thorn spines are noticeably enlarged, and it seems as if in this confusion of suffocating vapours, it seeks to pierce the sun itself.

Since the day I met Ilir, after coming from his last exhibition, I had not seen him in the city, and he did not answer the phone either. The door of his house was locked, and for the first time since I had known him, I did not know whether he had left town and, if so, why had he not given any notice, as he usually did on such occasions. Of course, I was worried beyond measure. The only thing that comforted me was a telegram he had sent to his sisters, telling them that he was busy working on a very important artistic production and that they would not hear from him for a while. I thought of his work at hand, of which he had spoken so passionately to me last time, and that helped me chill out, considering that you never know how artistic intuition will bait one to answer his higher calling and to chase the bags to recreate himself over and over again. And in order to achieve such a goal, complete detachment from previous routines, even if it means severing ties with friends and relatives, is mandatory. However, I feared that the burden he had taken on was self-consuming, although he never shied away from a challenge, no matter how difficult it initially presented itself. Especially in the heat of the news about Besian.

The only place where the heat had not penetrated was the thick, cemented walls of the prison, where Besian had been transferred. As soon as I got the chance, I paid him a visit to where he was locked up: a medieval castle in the north of the country, which had become a prison. During the hottest days of the year, the walls in the cells were sweating by thousands of bubbles forming on its surfaces, which, by sliding down in rivulets, create patches of cracked and swollen plaster that reveal a myriad of colours from the coated paint over the years interpenetrating. When one walks down those corridors, so neatly drawn by mould and dampness, as the iron doors open and slam, creaking, it feels like you are walking down the corridor in an exhibition full of expressionist paintings. It's just that it wasn't the fine arts that brought the visitors together in that place. If in the world outside those walls, every human being of character was free to fully develop his talents; inside, apart from the fact that developing one's abilities was out of the question, vices or habits could only be developed in a fragmentary and deformed way. While I was waiting for Besian to come to the meeting room, and I saw the prisoners passing by, it struck me how the weight of the concrete walls and the unyielding iron bars had given most of the prisoners their rigid forms, carving in their faces a thousand-yard stare. While some others, who were firm on preserving the vivacity with which they had lived their life before coming to that place, very soon turned into beings without any form or content, like the weeds that defy the asphalt and sprout from corner to corner in the prison yard. A shred of their freedom those walls could never stifle.

When I met Besian after not seeing him for so long, I couldn't help but be struck by his radical alienation. I had never seen him so fat and stupefied. It looked like a heart had grown wickedly out of proportion inside a ribcage. His eyes sparkled when he saw me, but that joy was ephemeral. That spark of freedom came fading until it was completely extinguished, and his face was plastered with a pale layer of ghastly worry. His gaze pierced through me and wandered around the room, as if trying to pinpoint the traces of pain that echoed in his chest. I tried to cheer his heart up by telling him all kinds of adventures that we had gone through together since childhood, but the only reaction I could gain from him was an empty chuckle, which somehow expressed his protest and request that I should give up the attempt to attract his attention and make the situation he was in more bearable than it actually was. He affirmed and denied the questions I asked with a single movement of his head as if to let me know that he despised my tricks to hook him into a conversation. A monstrous inner claw snapped relentlessly, with mighty frustration, at every thread that kept him connected to the outside world, like a captain who, with full consciousness, has raised the sails of his ship towards the absorbing vortex of nothingness at the bottom of the ocean. He returned to the land of the living for a moment and spent some time chatting with me after I told him the story of when, one day, we had gone to swim in the river. After the first dip in the water, we were sitting down to eat breakfast under the rustling shade of a willow when the melodious sounds of the flute that Besian played so eagerly joined the sloshing noises of the river and the chirping of the birds, as if to remind him of the summer, that he had spent in the sheds, high on the alpage, a year ago. And as you can think of a kitten or a puppy playing with the perception of light in the surrounding environment, as the veil on its eye dissolves after birth, so did Besian feel like a city boy visiting the countryside for the first time. Once there, he got a kick out of every craggy rock he went to, every donkey or mule he rode, every dog or other livestock he had befriended, but what had surprised him the most and also intrigued him was why the shepherd who lived up on the mountain blew and disturbed the silence of the night with the sound of his flute. "Bright eyes are an exalted forehead's endowment." answered the shepherd when he asked him one day. And when Besian, bewildered, insisted on his own, telling him that by doing so he was attracting the attention of wild animals in the surrounding forest, the shepherd had replied that "...it was useless to try to hide, when the wolf has had the sheep's livers hanging around its neck the whole time. But the whole matter rested on whether he would bite it or accept it as an extension of his own body." And indeed, the chief sheepdog of the shed, the one who cared most for the safety of the flock, did not feed other than from the hand of the shepherd. In the village feasts and weddings, this dog had its privileged position at the head of the table and was treated with more respect than many of the guests who gathered there. However, during the night, an unconscious howl breached its peace, luring and urging it to go to the vast forest, to become one with nature, and to return to his genesis as once upon a time. The flute's melody managed to interrupt that wail with fits and starts, appealing to an impromptu duet.

Ah, God knows how much Besian needed those airy sounds that emanated from the holes of the flute to confront his demons in the cell!

Perhaps the whole setting surrounding him, a vault of repressed human emotions, would be galvanized by the vibrations that the pipe emits and consequently collapse by its own weight. Perhaps the only way to come to terms with the old world dying and to welcome a new one that is struggling to be born is to collapse in on oneself...

When the time for the visit was up, we parted without saying much but manfully, eyeballing one another and greeting farewell with a bow of the head. Then he slowly got up and shuffled away, almost shambling like a sluggish seal instructed to return to the cage after performing the circus act.

The wave of heat cheering the political movement with resounding echoes was also felt in the distant villages where Sherif lives. The road to his place passes through a dense oak forest with semi-tall shrubs. The base path consists of black soil, where countless tree roots on both sides of the shoulders intertwine on the surface, as if nature had become bored with the world above and had begun to weave a new one from the underground. Plain as a pikestaff, it is an untrodden ground, which is threatened to be swallowed up entirely by the luxuriant vegetation on either side if, within a few months, there is no traffic along it. The crowns of the trees and the roots connect together, making the space between them take a funnel-shaped trajectory, like a constellation's narrow passage.

As you travel via this route, the rays of the sun breach through into the interior, amid the rustling and trembling of the leaves not entirely without struggle, splashing everything around with golden showers of twinkling lights. Wandering through this radiant channel gave the feeling of moving inside a giant kaleidoscope displaying the most wonderful forms and colours, where undoubtedly prevailed the relaxing green, the rippling blue of the depths, and the brilliant overlapping yellow. If you were walking on that trail at dusk, you could easily go off the rails and lose your way. And that forest would most likely turn into a deadly maze. At its end, behind the innumerable branches of tree ridges, the rocky foot of a mountain rises like the grey horizon of a stormy sky, which, because of the sparse vegetation, has been named the Bare Mountain.

Sherif had chosen to live in a glen of a few acres wide that was located between steep slopes, in a solitary lodging far from the inhabited areas. With the slates and stones that were in abundance around, he had built a two-story house, the walls of the second floor being part of the roof itself in the shape of an upside-down V.

The sun basked the plateau from dawn to sunset, and the tall crags that tower defiantly to the north and southeast protect it from the raging winds, giving the place an atmosphere of its own, different from the surrounding areas. The microclimate that enveloped the plateau blessed the soil with vegetables and fruits for growing in every season of the year. But above all, the grass was special. It rose with long green threads more than half a meter, swirling from the gust that blows from the slopes, the same as the grass on the bottom of the sea under the water currents. It was a miniature barn for Sherif's livestock, which consisted of a few heads of cattle, to meet his own ends.

That day, once I arrived there, a fascinating sight spread out before me, where a thunder-boomer bursts forth with rage, coughing out wind and firebolts on the mountain, while the latter holding its peace, unstirred by the lightning that was discharging on it, picked up all the drops of rain that fell, as if it were the petals of calendula, arranging it to gurgling serpentine lines of watersheds, gaining streams along the way, and feeding the brook. All of this happened from heights and shelters that could not be seen from down the valley where I was standing because layers of clouds like cotton were swirling vehemently around the slopes of the mountains. You could just about hear the rush of the water falling away toward the plunge basin, burbling and resonating, as it surged and collided against the rocks in the steep and sudden bends in the shape of the elbow. A portion of this stream Sherif had adapted into a tank to farm fish. Although it was possible to guddle it by the dozens, he still preferred angling it one at a time to amuse himself. The whole surrounding nature invites you to a pastoral dialectic, and in that state of contemplation, I found Sherif, who, leaning against the haystack, after periods of calmness, was interpolating with an intoning voice, addressing the precipitations of the clouds with gesticulations and shouts.

When he saw my facial features suddenly appear from the bushes, he stopped for a moment, furrowing his eyebrows from a distance, and when he was convinced that it did not belong to some curious wild animal that had come thick and fast from the woods, he was glad beyond measure. Apart from it and the shade of a technician who passed across to reach the location where the antennas are gathered, Sherif did not meet a living soul out there. And this was his conscious choice. After having a hard-knock life, a natural isolation room, like the plateau where he lives, is far better than a human prison. Approaching and cheerfully greeting him from a distance, Sherif signalled me to hush. His shoes were dirty with country slush, and his clothes as baggy as sacks of straw, his bulging eyes had popped out of their sockets as never before, and his prune like face, taking on all kinds of shapes every time he spoke and altered his facial expression, forming topographical maps of the most diverse genera, gave him a scowling and harsh appearance. He resembled an old bookseller who had the leaves of the trees for his library and every breathing creature in that place. In particular, he was very anxious that the patch of tranquillity he was cultivating on that plateau should not be disturbed by anyone except the sounds vibrating from the surrounding environment, which he seemed to absorb into his bosom, like the red spot on Jupiter, which consumes everything within it, in a cum sole motion.

Sherif was convinced that nature was not deceptive, unlike his previous experiences with the snares of the law conspiring against free spirits to condemn them with eternal damnation for deviating from the standard. Nature, for him, was a "living" dirt. Since you could not completely master its essence, you could at least communicate with it, just as an emigrant communicates with his past in the society from which he has been uncoupled and to which he can no longer go back due to the impossibility of distance, or where he is no longer welcome having fallen prey to certain circumstances. And if a feature of a thing or phenomenon was not as one might have thought at first, it was not because the natural phenomenon had duped him, for a phenomenon itself was transformed, in infinite succession, while he could follow and understand a certain phenomenon only in a fragmentary way. To fill the gaps created, he felt that his lame angle of view had to be constantly modified. He was resolved that the least he could do was to set all previous approaches at naught in order to adopt a pristine view. Only in this way could he grasp the primary object, the world as it was when its first perceptions started to get etched in his mind, and by doing this, to acquire from it brand new qualities that he had not noticed before.

According to him, one should speak only if he managed to match the spiritual pneuma within himself with the phenomena around him. This was the urge for the thought to become one with the object or phenomenon it seeks to perceive, even though the thought itself and the object may be indistinct at first. It is getting one's rhythm, evermore enriching and refining it in a duet of self and other. Is the initiation of processing thought towards an object or ambiguous phenomenon the beginning of humanity itself? Was the unquenchable thirst for clarity when faced with "false" natural phenomena the first impulse that excited prehistoric man?

This I cannot answer, but I know beyond doubt that on that plateau Sherif was a brute who consumed silence. He was completely infatuated with it. And here I'm not talking about the silent treatment of two kids when they "sulk" over a momentary bickering, but about the pure and thick silence that we first encounter in the presence towards our being and the world around it. For Sherif, silence was the medium where objects and phenomena took their forms. As many times as he recollected the first encounter with an object or phenomenon, he noticed something in it that had slipped his mind before. The silence was like the soil where the roots of memories and thought branched out, and with the passing of time, more buds opened. Like the ambush of an army that made the spoils of war sweeter the longer the war lasted. Who knows how many new phenomena the blood feud avenger noticed while waiting to ambush the wrongdoer?! How much new knowledge has he learned, when the event did not turn out according to his expectations?

Silence was a partner with whom he had lived for long enough. He breathed with it. He slept, dreamed and woke up with it. He knew its knacks. Usually, it did not make him feel like a mushroom. Even when it worked a trick or two on him, it did it with the good intention not to let him wander in the reflection of swampy appearances but to try to master an event to its fullest.

Silence for him was like the hidden gaze of a predator stalking him through the forest. When he thought quietly over himself, time would take another leap and transform his body into a giant coiled snail shell, where the swell waves of the sea foamed his being. When he thought silently about any object, he would turn it into any point in the endless ocean of space. Now, the silence and the mountain winds filled the void created when his mother departed, leaving him all alone in this world.

When the first rays of the sun darted tangentially across the firmament, Sherif took the drove road to the ben, chasing after the wind, like greased lightening Pegasus the whistle of Zeus, halting his gallop on the wellspring that flowed by the edge of a chasm, falling a little farther on, to form a thin plunge cataract. There, sweaty and scalded, he invigorated his silent muse with fresh water and clean, rare air, which pinched his lungs, and while he stood there, he thought about the past, the present and the future, life and death. For him, the latter was imagined as climbing up a mountain, where the higher you ascended, the less oxygen the air contained and the greater the fatigue, until it came to a point where the blessed death with its kiss suspended every biological process, thus completing the cycle of life.

And when not long had passed, while the sun completed the castling with the mountain slopes, and in between discerned Sherif's sweaty back, he would sigh and simultaneously spin on his heel to complete the cycle of oblivion, beginning a new day. In the evenings, after lighting the hearth, he would relax sitting on top of goat skins by the floor next to it and, at the same time, amused himself by harking to the intonation of voices and the oratory of various speakers on the radio. He especially gave heed to the world's literature anthology programs. There, he discovered characters with whom he shared common values and experiences, and this was his way of overcoming negative energies and being filled with hope.

He preferred listening to literary works rather than

reading them, ever since his life had been confined behind the bars of a cell and the fences of the internment camp. Reading had come to bore and disgust him, a reaction rooted in the days he was forced to flip through and recite state propaganda as part of his so-called re-education. But he loved the radio even more — it reminded him of the times he passed coded messages to fellow prisoners. The voices from the device echoed the signals they once tapped to each other through the darkness and silence of the isolation chambers. Those messages were the only window of communication with the other fellow suffering inmates.

When the stillness became an indigestible plume for his soul, Sherif would descend into the city, wandering through its streets and blending into the dense flow of people and traffic. On the main boulevard, amidst the crowd, his soul seemed to dissolve into the thousand and one stories unfolding around him. For a fleeting moment, his gaze would follow the wheels of a passing bicycle. Then, he'd purse his lips as the creak of a machete blade echoed, sinking into flesh, sending trickles of blood across the face and sleeves of the butcher's white apron in the shop across the street. He felt the dreamy sensuality of two young people having a tryst leaning against the corner of a passion-pit stairwell, chewing face. His eyes would trail the erratic path of a schoolboy dashing down the street, backpack swinging wildly, while his friends chased after him, cheering.

In this haunted, drifting state, Sherif would roam until the heat, generated by the friction between the thin soles of his shoes and the asphalt, rose through his feet, swelling them. At that moment, he would stop and feel strangely alive and at ease, as though he had stood still all along, and it was the ground itself that had been slipping beneath his feet.

Sherif keeps recounting how he spent his life in solitude wearing a smile. During my visit to his place, our conversations burned as vividly as the hearthflame, flickering and licking our faces with its fiery tongue. The echoes of our laughter would curl upward, creeping along the mountain's neck before scattering into the sky, quicker even than the smoke billowing from the chimney.

In the same manner, the city spun around its axis in those days, like a flaming globe balanced on the tip of a dictator's finger.

*   *   *

When the burden of being becomes unbearable, and troubles pour down with the sudden fury of a cloudburst, a spiritual sigh escapes the chest and lingers in the air, like a final bequest that roams restlessly through the hearts of loved ones as a family member lies in the last throes of life. Such is the atmosphere everywhere on the eve of electoral silence, just days before citizens cast their votes. The promises made during the campaign are plastered on posters affixed to poles, walls, and any available surface in the streets, while the airwaves, radio and television alike, echo with slogans so grandiose and sweeping they make the biblical Flood sound like a children's tale. And while at first glance, many of these slogans appear contradictory. Yet in truth, they are all branches of the same laurel crown — the winner's crown.

Society, as if embodied in a single abstract form, holds its breath for a moment. According to ritual and tradition, it escorts the past, the yesterday that still chokes back its final sobs, toward its last resting place. In doing so, it celebrates the birth of novelty, the promise of something new blooming on its lips, casting its reflection onto the uncertain horizon of the future.

Under normal circumstances, people who would have nothing to do with each other are gathering en masse in the hotel these days to consult with Pasqualino. It is his skill in swaying interest groups among the common folk and stirring ideas even in the most barren of souls, combined with Mrs. Bekteshi's charm in drawing them in, that has roused most of them from their lethargic slumber and pulled them out of their lair in a typical local pub.

A few of the supporters linger by the entrance, smoking and chattering idly. Some others, as they sip their coffees, take notes on the chronicle coverage that journalists have devoted to the political and social situation in the country. Among them are also those who mill around the electoral campaign headquarters conference room observing the latest directives and information for the teams stationed all over the country. Add to that the agile movement of the bar and restaurant staff; and one cannot help but sense the weighty, oppressive silence hanging in the air — like the depths of the sea, still and thick, while a storm rages above; a charged atmosphere which wraps itself around you as soon as one steps through the main entrance. So much has this electrifying current spread out its halls that it is not necessary to fold a corner of the newspaper sheet while flipping the page, as it sticks to the finger as soon as the cheekbones touch it. Amidst this confusion, the candid face of Ermal, the cheeky porter, stands out while lugging two suitcases, politely addressing a throng of men gathered in the area in front of the elevator, asking them to clear their way from its doors "Dear guests, please, carry yourselves a little further, cause' I'm not able to belly up to the bar." he says, while sweat beads up on his forehead.

"We just arrived here today from the city L." sputters one of them, a man in his forties, who is holding a large file in his hands, "Here we have the pleading request from the residents of the city of L., who are convinced to the point of self-sacrifice regarding the issue raised by Mrs. Bekteshi in the meeting a week ago." He concludes excitedly and full of self-satisfaction with the posture of someone showing his loyalty to his superior during a military parade.

"I comprehend you down to the tiniest detail," Ermal addresses them with aplomb "but this is not a place suited for political rallies. You can stay here until you are called forth and over and done with your business while the rest of you, gents, can you please wait outside? If you may, of course."

"Ah, most certainly, right away. I apologize! All this mess comes as a result of the long hours that we have travelled today without taking a rest, so much so that we no longer discern anything, or we know where we are for that matter. That's how exhausted we are. Once more, I am truly sorry." he finishes and bids the others to go outside. Ermal thanks him, greets him, and, as if he were a robot powered by batteries, lifts the suitcases he had temporarily left on the ground and walks toward the exit, where a yellow taxi waits with the trunk wide open.

The door to the meeting room swings open suddenly, revealing Pasqualino's glabrous face, his cheeks flushed a rosy hue. It is evident he has just concluded a spirited exchange with a group of young people, whom he now escorts towards the main exit. And after amicably parting with them, he waves to the delegates from city L Then, turning left, he throws a cheeky wink at a cluster of people gathered by the bar — at the same time catching my eye and giving me a wave. I had just come off the first shift at the hotel, and we all made our way inside.

From the effortless finesse he displayed in that moment, one could hardly argue he hasn't perfectly mastered Mrs Bekteshi's mannerisms in his dealings with the public.

If, out in the hall and beyond the hotel, the very air was so charged that it made one's hair stand on end as energy passed from person to person, then inside the meeting room, it felt as though a furious thrush were beating against one's chest with the precision of Hephaestus's hammer. Every object in the room seemed to be locked in competition — not only with each other but with the people themselves — to claim as much space as possible.

Outside, dense clouds — like a fustanella flung across the firmament — drift restlessly as frosty white air masses. The hazy, slender rays that drizzle through them strike the windowpane and, with effort, filter into the room, unable to fully saturate the objects within with light or gleam. The lustred brown walnut table standing in the middle, the central part of which is in the shape of a rectangle, and its rounded sides in the shape of a semi-arch, resembles a plot of artificial plants made of wax, from which notebooks, pens, water bottles, glasses, fruit plates and a tinsel chandelier are sprouting up under and over it.

Directly opposite the table stands a large wooden wall clock, its light honey-coloured frame and pendulum lending it a quiet dignity. In the dullest, most airless moments of the meeting — when the speakers' voices grow ever more monotonous, like muffled echoes drifting from deep within a cave, the pendulum seems to transform into a censer in a clergyman's hand, swinging solemnly back and forth across the room.

To the left, opposite the window, sits a small table draped in a white tablecloth. Atop it, sugar cubes are neatly stacked beside porcelain cups, and three thermoses; one filled with tea, the other two with coffee.

Behind Pasqualino stands a board propped on three tall iron poles, curled at their ends, upon which keywords and numerous colour schemes of the most varied kind could be seen. Yet what most strongly conveys the sense of confinement and stifling atmosphere in the room are the immense, weighty curtains of cherry-coloured silk, so thick they might just as well be mats suspended from frames, and the shaggy, tufted carpet of muted red, which retains the imprint of footsteps long after someone has stood or passed across it.

While everyone sits down, Pasqualino asks for the window shutters to be opened in order to get rid of the breathless stale air that had accumulated in the warm stuffy room from the previous meetings, where from the new opening created a couple of houseflies, which just a few moments ago were buzzing and creaking like a dry pumpkin, as they stubbornly battered against the windowpane, seized their chance and made a swift escape into the open air.

Overall, twenty-five individuals occupy the room, each tasked with coordinating the central election office with its local branches across every district. At the head of the table sits Pasqualino, and to his right stands Karl, bearing the ever-shifting grimace of a loyal footman, perpetually chewing on processed tobacco. What renders his features all the more indeterminate—and, indeed, perplexing— is the evident inner conflict as to whose whims he ought to serve: those of the hotel director, who has remained conspicuously absent from everyone's view for quite some time, and likely will continue to do so; or Pasqualino, who has fed him promises of a hopeful future.

Next to him, directly across from me, stood three girls dressed in flowing white dresses adorned with pink flowers. From the cut and stitching of their garments, to their faces powdered like geishas and their hair pinned back with a pencil, its shaft bearing three different colours, serving as a makeshift hair stick, it was difficult to discern whether they were friends, sisters, or triplets. Whatever their relation, what bound them together like beads on a nylon thread was the muffled, ever-present chorus of giggles that escaped whenever one of us spoke while at the same time attempting to veil their laughter behind hands as slender as cherry twigs, making it impossible to tell which of them was laughing at any given moment.

Further along the side, a line of "anonymous overcoats and thick sideburns" stands in silent attendance, as if plucked from the prop store of some bygone theatrical production, left behind like relics by the company at the end of their tour. Whether the dark glasses they wear serve to shield their eyes from meeting ours, or whether they are blind — or perhaps hypersensitive to light — I can not say. They seem far more intent on eavesdropping, tracking the echo of our voices as it drifts across the room, often averting their gaze from the speaker to fix upon some dark or desolate corner. These are Mrs Bekteshi's staunchest followers, her true blue representatives, who spoke little, if at all, throughout the proceedings.

Next to me stood a professor of economics with swollen cheekbones and a frozen, stiff lower jaw, who inflicted on himself a great deal of pain every time he tried to speak because the upper part of the jaw and, with it, the whole head, shook and opened like the drawbridge of a castle, while the back of the neck was twisted with convulsions.

This was the only way he could squeeze even a single sound out of his organism. Thus, he was forced to speak through his teeth all the time. And, bearing in mind this anomaly, it would be impossible to comprehend any word he uttered were it not for his assistant always standing beside him, a young man of about thirty, with fair spiky hair and a head like a brush, with the lower part of the jaw in the shape of a horseshoe, that bobbed up and down as if someone was pulling it by the goatee when he spoke. One may well account him as a puppet of the professor, who spoke with his stomach while the assistant carefully dubbed the words one by one, his voice barely rising in intonation.

Behind them stands a once-prominent politician, his noble features still discernible: a high forehead, a slightly menacing crooked nose, and thin, serene lips which he habitually rubbed together as he pondered or prepared to respond, an obvious attempt to bolster his self-esteem and buy time in order to convey his personal interests as effectively as possible. The only flaw in his appearance is his rather long thigh paired with thin, unmuscular legs, which made him resemble a disoriented frog stranded on dry land whenever he ventured to the beach. Yet, clad in wide flare trousers and seated, he projects the image of a stoic giant, one who might challenge even the god's lightning bolt to achieve his aims. Cast adrift and rejected by the party he once led, he is now intent on bequeathing the art of politics to his son, a weirdo collector who had first indulged his passions in childhood by pinning butterflies, and as he grew, turned to amassing properties. Were it still legal, he might well continue collecting slaves to this day. The father sought to endow his heir with the ability to command militants, mobs, and voters alike, and, if fortune favoured him, to once again seize the gilded throne of party chairman with his claws. His old instincts, honed in the corridors of power, whispered in his ear that it was better to be the chairman anywhere, even in prison, than second in command anywhere else.

Other seats along the row are taken by former merchants, industrialists, and bankers who were rolling in it and, fed up with the success of money-making, were now hoping that their green folding staff would earn them a place in the celebration picture on the historical-political chronicle of the country.

Sitting in the back rows is the man clutching the request-prayer file from City L., whom Ermal had encountered earlier in the hall.

After casting a passing glance at the three unripe lasses, who scarcely stifle their chuckling, Pasqualino pipes up and thunder "Ciamar gob gaffawer bonny puss lass?"

We had known for a while that Pasqualino hailed from the diaspora. We'd often heard him growl at himself in that tongue—a language that felt as curiously familiar as it was foreign and indecipherable. But this was the first time he had addressed anyone else in it directly—and even more so in front of everyone else.

Perhaps his anxious state is also related to the fact that last night, he and Mrs. Bekteshi, after a meeting with the party supporters, were invited to a local fiesta steeped in pagan rites held in the rural area, where after polishing off several crates of wine and skewering a dozen cattle along with a few piglets, while tearing up the dance floor, almost setting it alight, they burned the bachelor's handkerchiefs, that were flung in the air here and there over the heads of people like flaming comets. The festivities later spilled into the outer courtyard, where dances were organised, jumping over fires lit with scraps found in the surroundings. Pasqualino, while on a beer blast, had stripped off his shirt and set it alight, whirling it in the air around his head like a gorilla celebrating his coronation as the king of the forest. That the same night, he was almost crowned as Mrs. Bekteshi's *amore*, when lusting after her in a libidinal craze, he had kissed her likeness appearing on the glass pane in the hall of mirrors, at the city amusement park on the street E., where they wandered for a few hours after the party.

The agony became even more searing when he was escorting Mrs. Bekteshi back to the hotel, expecting to steal from her —at the very least— a good night kiss, but apart from the reddish-purple marks on his cheeks, there was a last one added on his forehead, as the door slammed on his face, giving him the final blow for that night, with the housekeepers of the hotel finding Pasqualino next morning sprawled on the floor outside her door. Yet for him—who had clearly bitten off more than he could chew—, this occasion was a testimony of the lunatic love that tortured her conservative soul, which, according to the custom, before letting him keep your heart, you must first see how the man you will have forever by your side reacts being let go.

At this sudden outburst, our attention, mixed with misunderstanding and curiosity, is focused on Pasqualino. It is the only moment when the girls stop laughing up their sleeves. Grave silence would have sealed the meeting with its heavy cloak if Karl, who, smiling faintly and contemptuously, did not intervene to tell us that Pasqualino had merely asked "If the ladies were done with their full of grace laughter?"

This time, a volley of laughter resonates along with the hair and bits of paper fluttering with the breeze in the room while it is being vented. Karl, ever the polyglot prodigy that he is, had mastered in a few months the syntactic structures and the basic vocabulary of an archaic language, such as the one with which Pasqualino expressed himself in the moments when life brought a lump to his throat, so that there would be no obstacle in communication between him and Pasqualino. While noticing the latter's weakness for Mrs. Bekteshi, as well as her closeness to Behar, he volunteered to poke his nose, collect information on the relationship of the pair, and inform him of every move that the two of them made.

Only Pasqualino maintained his stoic resolve, and when the laughter died away, he stood up straight and tall, his right hand clutching the top of the suit's lapels and his bleary eyes gazing upwards outside, musing by the window as if a celestial whirlwind was threatening to slang him out from that room any second, hinting from the strained features of his face, that the discourse he was about to deliver was perhaps the most important of the whole campaign.

"Dear political creatures — and indeed, we are political creatures— as long as we assemble, deliberate and then disperse to act, only to gather once more. Or isn't that so?!" he asks, breaking his engagement with the outside world and focusing his look on us, and receiving our tacit approval, he presses on "I have chosen to keep in direct contact with each one of you individually throughout this time since I wanted our goals, our way of organization, as well as the chain of command to be as secure as possible from any information leakage, that could harm our endeavour, and derail our campaign. But now that only a few days separate us from the election's silence, let's open all the cards, and may the best team win.

To begin with, let me regale you with a story that will give us a better understanding of the current situation we are in. This is the chronicle of an army whose mission was to reach the farthest ends of the earth. It was convinced that it could only be achieved through justice because only by meticulously following this road could they hope to move forward without wandering eternally in the labyrinth of past mistakes, which were essentially the same. However, from time to time, those same mistakes still materialised in different kinds of shapes and forms.

To avoid the previous corrupt practices, they decided to march only in a straight line, where none other than the most faithful advisers of all generations, the stars, would be their guiding light. And one of the postulates that flashed on their way announced that from a fair exchange, all emerge victorious — for the salt borne to the highlands is worth as much as the milk brought down from the pastures to the seashore.

What's more, in times gone by, many other armies have tried the same feat, only to fail, as greed, lust and impotence seized them along the way, and as a result, they capitulated as degenerates, disintegrating without a trace.

The soldiers, officers, and commanders of the army I am speaking of felt like bear cubs whose burning desire drove them to emerge from their den for a stroll, the same as they used to do as toddlers when any novel sound or smell invited them to an enlightenment dance of the world around. But stepping beyond their natural environment meant stepping, inevitably, into the natural environment of somebody else's cave, where in order to connect and communicate with cubs that dwelled there, one first has to come face to face with the she-bear that guarded their space. And the wildest and most fearsome bear they had ever encountered was the she-bear of their own homeland's shared spaces, which was crystallized by the twinning of all the bearesses in the surrounding area. As a result of this interweaving, the personification of the patron deity of the city was created as a symbiosis, where the ideal union of everyone's mothers would act as each one's arch-matron. And as the army marched onward, it came up against numerous other militias. Bloody battles took place, where, either thanks to their abilities or to luck, in any case, fortune favoured them as the brave. But being victorious for them meant twinning themselves with the cubs there, which could not be achieved without first twinning the respective she-bears of the common spaces. So, with each step forward, they offered the finest of their own culture and received the best of the culture they met along the way. Thus, days, months, and years passed, and they were exalted with virtues and knowledge, as well as the spoils of war that they had acquired, riches of a kind never before imagined in their homeland. And yet, the ultimate goal — the discovery of the earth's farthest edge — had not yet been accomplished, and there seemed to be no end in sight.

Until one day, exhausted but not disheartened in their original quest to find the ends of the earth, they suddenly realised they had arrived at the very point from which their journey had begun. This caused fear and uncertainty. The once impeccably disciplined lines started to disintegrate, and the soldiers began to defy the commands they had previously followed so blindly. The bewilderment, despair, and misunderstanding that followed brought about the first schism, where one party argued that it was impossible for them to have erred, for they had followed the directions instructed by the stars with the utmost exactitude, while the other party insisted that if the instructions had been followed so diligently, then there was no way that they would have ended up at the same place from where they had started.

So, from the first big rift, fights, disagreements and murders between the conflicting factions were soon to follow. That once united army of self-astery, which had set out in pursuit of the earth's final frontier, ended up divided into bitterly polarised camps, each fighting the other to the death to reclaim the former glory. And finding the middle third, when the parties were so polarized, would have been as improbable as finding the far ends of the earth had it not been for a chubby soldier who had never once omitted plum jam from his breakfast menu since it was recommended to him in a distant land for stamina while marching. He couldn't bear to see the carnage unfolding in front of his eyes, prompting him to advise the conflicting sides that if the earth was round and not flat, as they had assumed it until then, this might be one of the possibilities as to why they had returned to their point of departure.

From that day forth, the quarrelling ceased, and they resolved henceforth to part ways and wander on solitary journeys to the four winds to find out the farthest reaches and all that was to be discovered on earth, which might well be a sphere after all, and decided to meet once in a while to discuss any novelties they had come up against throughout their individual campaigns.

This is the situation we find ourselves in. " there is a pregnant silence, and Pasqualino begins to slouch around the room. At the same time, two of the "anonymous thick-sideburns" are thrown into the mode of locomotion, imitating him in every move he made, accompanied in the background by the sneaky giggling of the mischievous girls as they are watching a potbelly waiter changing the thermoses of coffee and tea.

"So, as I was saying," he resumes his speech, "I would like us to be those bears who enjoy plum jam for breakfast, as well as marching towards the furthest edge of the earth. And here I am not talking about the geographical edge, but rather the edge of the heart. The kind of heart capable of overcoming the divisive force of the self. How many of you here today have truly feasted with the people, with the ordinary folk?"

"In the district where I oversee the campaign's progress, we've organised supper for the poor and needy on numerous occasions," intervenes the politician who has been ousted from his party.

"You are not grasping my point, dear friend, while you of all people should have been the first to comprehend me correctly, as an old wolf in the political arena that you are. speaking of the alms, nor chilli and beans provided to the destitute, or to the foster and retirement homes, but to sit cross-legged and loaf dip at each other's bowls, sharing laughter, tears, and song. It's the only way to get to know — and twin with — the bear of the common spaces. If you manage that, you'll come to understand what people fear, what disheartens them in their daily lives. It is this cognitive and creative process that serves our purpose of gaining power."

"We settled this issue long ago," broke in a corpulent industrialist, his sagging cheeks wobbling with every word. The black horn-rimmed spectacles perched lightly on the tip of his nose were employed solely for perusing the many documents before him, while he locked his gaze on the faces of the interlocutors by looking directly at them over his glasses. His black liquid equine eyes with short eyelashes seemed as if they were filled with oil impurities and metal rust from where the ink dripped, soaking his pen, which flowed smoothly, keeping notes.

"The postulate of the stars in our galaxy says that the more we postpone our payments for suppliers and wages, as well as for our products across distribution points, the healthier the balance sheet."

"By all means. The time value of money and its liquidity are very important." agreed a banker, clad in crimson trousers and a checkered blazer, a turquoise scarf knotted round his neck — its brilliance rather pitiful, like the jingle of gold coins in a beggar's palm.

"While for us merchants, selling a comb to a bald-headed man is the pinnacle of our craft." chimed in a businessman with pride, dressed in breeches with suspenders, wearing Wellington boots, and had a raincoat draped over his shoulders, which made him look like the Lord of the Scrapyard.

"Daddy, Daddy, why don't you fetch the right answer to them? You have always been a walking encyclopedia for me." the son of the politician intervenes, who lost his sense of whereabouts in that polyphony of ideas.

At last, the dolorous professor's jaw-clenching is heard and interpreted into comprehensive terms by his assistant, stressing that adhering to industry best practices remained the wisest course of action.

"I fail to see how simply hampering the circulation of money and accumulating it in a single hand, like in a poker game, is a solution in the long term." seeking a clearer understanding of his intentions.

"To begin with, you have to watch out and distinguish between the two types of circulation. There is the circulation of goods in the industry, and another circulation that is harder to grasp and more abstract, which is that of money itself." the banker intervenes, "This latter form, you see, came about as a necessity to facilitate the exchange of goods, ideas and, inevitably, the cultural products of one society. I'm not entirely certain how realistic this comparison I'm just about to demonstrate now is, but in the spirit of making it more digestible for you, I would liken the circulation of goods to the cardiovascular system, and the circulation of money to the body's nervous system. The latter has grown ever more complex, due to the change in the human organism itself. Some functions or entire organs may stop performing, and others may take over the same functions, or new organs may come into being."

"For me, amassing large amounts of liquid assets is beneficial, as the surplus can be invested in brand-new machinery to increase the percentage of return on capital employed." the industrialist reinforced his opinion, "In fact, the more employees I can replace with automation systems, the more profitable it will be for me in the long run."

"Yes, without a doubt, if your products were used by robots instead of humans, it would be so much better." sardonically replied one of the "anonymous thicksideburns".

"And I who thought that medieval tortures were all past and gone. As a starter, make them feeble by not paying their salary on time to put food on the table, and then throw them in the mass graveyard of unemployment." intervenes an "anonymous jacket".

"In fact, the second case should be conceived as a stimulation or incitement of an organ, then circulation, so that it finds its place within the whole." the banker elaborates further, "As well as the other way around, the impetus which a particular organ transmits to the whole to let it know how it assumes its purpose, and what resources it needs to optimize its functionality. So, money, just like the nervous system, so to speak, transmits secondary impulses through the entire organism to its individuals, being derived from the source itself, that of the vitality of life. But this superconducting 'gadget', although it is just a dummy, is of the same nature as the source because, without it, it would not be possible to glister its rays all the way, the night traveller taking care to guide."

"Ha, ha, ha, you bankers are such freewheeling spending fellas!" burst out the industrialist, "You fancy yourselves saints from the days when treasures were guarded in shrines and sanctuaries. But, if it weren't for us who produce and give shape and value to the whole jinbang, what use would your money be?! At most, to stick to the same ground of comparison, one might assign to money the role that plasma plays in the bloodstream, that, by increasing or decreasing its flow according to the economic and social organization conditions, does not let capital clot. However, placing the banking system on equal ground as the sense organ is like equating the banana handed to the monkey after a trick to the circus performer himself. For God's sake, straighten up yourselves."

"I implore you to keep both feet on the ground." a merchant jumps into the conversation, "If it weren't for me, the circus artist you are speaking about, who boggles people's minds urging them to purchase the whole shoot, among which items they have never heard of or will ever need, you two would still be swinging from the trees."

"Gentlemen," Karl joins the conversation, "I implore you to make a tiny effort and abandon your own grounds of narrow interests. You remind me of spoilt children, each boasting about whose toy is the prettiest the moment they're given one. And where would your businesses be without supervisors like myself, the 'Big Brother', so to speak, who keeps an eye on everything?! And who cares about the fate of a cog in the wheel of the economic settings of a society?! Your previous achievements are like that trifling cog. For you to grow and become the wrenches that tighten and loosen these cogs and possess the state machinery that performs these operations, you must embrace the public. For victory to be possible, we must think 'Macro'. Do you understand? 'Macro'!"

"Ah, 'Macro'!" the assistant's voice was heard, interpreting and making the professor's anguished sigh intelligible, now paired with the sound of his jaw clenching like a crown block engaging, "A marvellous subject indeed, which seeks to explain how the decrease or increase of one variable affects others and the economy as a whole throughout history. But what conditions in the present create the ideal state and incite the decision-making for the future it cannot say since what happened before is explained in a straight line of cause and effect. And decisions about the future spring to life in a dynamic and not static environment, as we would like to think about the past. And, it could not have been otherwise that the love of my life is the subject of finance accounting. I rear it as if it was my only child. But if I understood the speaker correctly, he is talking about the 'Macro' ground of standing, a broader view of the economic environment as a whole. I cannot but agree with him one hundred per cent."

"What 'Macro' ground of standing are you talking about!" cried the exiled politician, finally shaking off the sting of wounded pride from a few minutes earlier, "These

190

are nothing but palaver. The day-to-day problems and troubles people struggle with are 'Micro'. Spouting words like 'micro' and 'macro' only means you're speaking past them. Ordinary folk are concerned with the basic, essential matters of everyday life. The past slips from their memory faster than you can blink. If by 'Macro' you mean some grand, all-encompassing perspective on the population as a whole, let me tell you a little something from a few years back, when the party I led actually won the elections and took office. By the end of the mandate, for so many reasons, not only did we not build a better future, but we also blamed it on the prevailing socio-cultural condition of the time, which suggested that to discover something new, you had to first strip away the old, and since there is more than one way to skin a cat, whatever means you employ to achieve it, is well worth it. As such, among other things, we advocated explosives as the most guaranteed way to achieve this end. For example, when the fishing industry hit choppy waters, we recommended the use of dynamite in the body of water to increase production. When the black gold and mining industry was in trouble, we again called for more explosive power to blast the earth to smithereens and bring the so precious mother lode to the surface, like the grain overeaten by the donkey, when its guts are split open from rapture. Was there something wrong in the energy sector? 'Boom!' More explosives! Even the curtains in the theatre or cinema hall were torn apart with fireworks just to get the show started. So much so that you couldn't open a door or crack a window without a gram of C4. Not to mention our roaring away during the public outings, which would make even the most agelast executioner tremble with fear. Even more so, the children, who quaking like an aspen leaf, collapsed into their parents' laps and offering up their milk teeth, 'so that the notorious gaffer wouldn't jump out from the TV screen and pull it out with pincers'. By the end of the term in office, I was an expert in the subject of improvised explosive devices. When the only thing left to blow up was one's brain, I grabbed whatever I could get my hands on from the state's treasury and made away while the crowd followed me behind. And the most beautiful thing is that the crowd had no consciousness whatsoever but was simply a formless mass, gushing forth into the street like the solidifying wave of lava from a volcano, as a perpetuation in the cultivation of stagnation of my latest profession.

And when the next day they asked me why I was fleeing like a coward with my tail between my legs, I told them that I was racing on the world marathon course, which takes place between the greatest civilizations, but you can't understand a thing, because you focus on irrelevancies. And the crowd bought it. Ah, 'Macro'. Ah, the crowd. What a damp squib!"

"Daddy, daddy, will I be able to use the chainsaw to put asunder the crowd this time, the one you bought me for my birthday last year? Please, dad, since I am bothered blasting people with explosives, as you lose the part of the languishing, the pleading and the departing of the soul. You know, father, that I am studying where souls go after they separate from the body so that when that day comes, I may know how to return and to become immortal, as we deserve to be."

"Haven't these politicians and their minions yet understood that, from the times of Ancient Egypt, the only way to become immortal is to embalm the body, turning it into a mummy?!" muttered an 'anonymous thick-sideburn' to his fellow next to him, "If this process is carried out while the body is still alive, even better." answers the other, "In this way, the preservation of the body in time is guaranteed."

"Yes and no." says the first speaker, "It rather depends on what you mean by it. If, for instance, someone else, an opponent, for example, forces you to perform such an act of self-embalming, as a form of dissent, perhaps for moral or religious reasons, or such an act is carried out in protest against some edict imposed by the social environment in which you live, as it contradicts the values that your character enshrines, or his opponent performs this ritual against someone still living, placing them unwillingly on the pedestal of eternity, then yes, it does make sense. But to perform this act, both towards yourself and towards others, because, like a dictator, you want to predetermine your own death or that of others because your ego wants to elevate itself on the pedestal of eternity, then for sure something is deeply amiss."

Meanwhile, Pasqualino casts a sheep's eye on us every now and then as to suggest that were it not for Mrs Bekteshi, we'd stand no chance of even entering the electoral contest, let alone winning it.

"Honourable Gentlemen who have gathered here today. Using explosives is not the right way, and even less so is withholding the wages of the employees in order to manage cash flow. Above all, it is inhuman. Particularly so when it becomes the standard that all the other enterprises must follow. This is an unfair and enslaving competitive advantage. In my opinion, in addition to the optimal utilization of resources, one should also consider substitute and alternative options. The belt may be pulled a notch or two, but if you overtighten the purse strings, you risk asphyxiating the entire organism.

Regarding the economy, we will have time later to clarify the details better; it is a long and intricate debate in which the discussion of the psycho-cultural values and properties of goods and services in a society is intertwined with the experimental quantitative variables of the economy that may be controlled. Moving from the qualitative argument of the goods and services to that of quantitative inevitably affects the way we see and understand these values of products and services that we create, causing the debate to start all over again and everything to be reconsidered from scratch.

But I have gathered you here tonight to talk about institutional policies since the general elections serve precisely to renew the offices that hold such a power, where economic policies undoubtedly play an irreplaceable role.

Aren't the institution's public spaces like caverns, where the cries of the past generation reverberate, forming a reality, a matter in which the dreams of the young generation, as a pure creative and perpetual energy, collide, constantly altering it? Aren't the symbols and messages forged within it a flaming torch, sparkly particles of the faces of the fathers, like a chronicle of the past, drawing the attention of the next generation, as if speaking to itself back in time about the journey it had to take to this very day and the unexpected, miscalculations and errors, that have occurred along this journey, dregs which are entrusted to us to straighten up before we start our own voyage? Aren't their voices wandering in the public institutions under the guise of the 'Other', since to be able to send a message to someone in another time and space, even to oneself, the ego has to split and reconcile under the guise of the 'Other', alienating itself in the process, as a leap from and a returning to itself?

There is a word in Ancient Greek that is used interchangeably with the term 'Public', that perfectly encapsulates what I mean to express. That word is 'Proksenos', which translates as 'Aye to foreigners', meaning a message approved and agreed for the foreigners. This is the language of the law, or rather, the institutional tongue. It is a stiff language that tries to speak in time to all generations. But this language derives from the amorphous substance cultivated by the people and aims to return to it again, where it will finally rest in peace in the form of services, only to reawaken from it as a social necessity.

And for us to be represented in these institutions, we must bring with us at least a modest degree of innovation, we must bring with us at least a modest degree of innovation. Only thanks to this innovation can we flatten the curve of lunacy of the past and outline the plan for the future. But to accomplish this, we must get to know as best as we can the psychic profiles of the individuals who make up the population and those who govern them so that we can learn their habits, desires, fears, superstitions, and beliefs, which must become ours too. And we have done a pretty good job so far, which is worth praising, but it is still not enough.

As we are running out of time, I want you all to crowd on sail and focus on the fears and the superstitions since, by exploiting those, we can connect more fundamentally with their way of thinking, reacting and living. Their greatest fears, terrors and spiritual oppressions will, in the days ahead, be your polar star, which you must address in the discourses you will hold in your respective districts. By tinkering around with these strings, you will initially cause panic to spread throughout the population. Then, by presenting solutions to those problems that you yourself indirectly raised, you will become heroes and saviours of the whole nation. Therefore, in the days ahead, in your public appearances, you should listen more than you should talk. You must make yourselves more accessible towards the general public, wire back to us the problems that the residents face, and offer them your solutions to these problems. Make sure your promises are feasible, short, and focused on the core of the problems, not their causal effects. In a word, from now until the date when the elections will be held, I want you to sing from the same hymn sheet and burn as a candle of invocation among the masses of the people. Your faces should be the first in which their spleen and the fervour of their prayers are vented." Pasqualino concludes and sits in his place.

At this point, the man from the city of L., holding the pledge file in hand stands up and stirred and inspired by Pasqualino's speech, begins to speak enthusiastically "Last week, at the rally held in our city by Mrs Bekteshi, she urged us to be more vigilant and to pursue, without hesitation, our shared goals of greater employment, as well as to draw up a plan in the form of an appeal for achieving this. And this is our petition, signed without exception by all the members of the party's group-section in the city L. We are convinced that our economic destitution and loss of moral value are a result of the world, the flesh, and the devil, which are induced by nightlife activity in the city. And as a remedy against it, we plan to launch a large balloon at twilight, bearing the image of a terrifying bunny with bloodshot eyes, tusks sharp as saw blades, and one ear bent, slightly bitten off. This balloon will overlap the moon along its trajectory from dusk till dawn. Its sweet rays will light the nimbus of a dreadful creature that flies through the sky and instil terror even in the bravest among us, everyone cowering away at home and not leaving until the morning, rested and fresh, ready to start a new day."

"Oh Lord," sighed Pasqualino between his teeth, "we will need a miracle to win this one."

The speeches and discussions went on. Despite the extended hours of the meeting, the sniggering of the mischievous lasses did not cease until we all left the room. Also unchecked went the behaviour and involuntary twitches of the "anonymous thick-sideburns and jackets", with the end of the meeting finding one of them hanging from the chandelier with his head down and his mouth wide open, trying to snatch a green apple from the fruit basket on the middle of the table.

*　　*　　*

Word on the wire is that we, the attendees, formed the nucleus of the movement. In truth, we are more like a cake, with Pasqualino as the cherry on top of it, to satisfy the appetites of Mrs. Bekteshi, who, it must be said, had sunk her teeth deep into the electoral campaign. One more failure would cause a nervous breakdown, which under these circumstances would have irreversible consequences. Perhaps not quite as dramatically as the emotional collapse she suffered upon resigning from the theatre, but could well prove serious and maybe insurmountable, considering her age. All the energy, experience and anger accumulated over the years, she radiated to each party member with her own pathetic compassion as an actress, cloaking each of us, some more so and some a little less in an aura that set us apart from the militants of the established parties, like a distinctive label that makes a product stand out on a crowded shelf. Each of us, Pasqualino and I included, had adopted something from her, whether it was the graceful motion of her hand that stilled a murmuring crowd at a rally when she took the stage. Or the times that she quietly and gracefully answered the cynical questions of some yellow journalist, as well as the sighs she let slip while describing the current living conditions of the inhabitants, or something in the same vein. All this made her a role model among us, where everyone felt represented in the harmonizing figure that she embodied. Her inspiration and ability to arm us with blind obedience to the political movement, which was gaining more popularity by day, had injected a dose of fear and trembling into the authority in power, who, in the last days of the elections, had lost touch with reality. This animating force, with which she inspired each of us, is best reflected in her schmooze but magisterial aperçu at the campaign's closing rally "…Have not today's high men on the pole turned into quixotic knights, seeking to yoke a monster, using thin threads as reins?! And justice turns into such a beast when some try to ride it for personal gain. And, thus, inevitably to the detriment of others.

When the principle of equality among the members of society is reduced into a mere statement that is uttered vaguely to justify the injustices of the past rather than to guarantee justice for the future, then we have paved the way for the corruption of the next generation. And, here I am not talking about the equality of being all the same, who eat the same and play the same, sleep the same and dream the same. What I mean is that everyone should have the same basket of opportunities, and according to their free will, they should make choices in life. If the possibilities in this basket do not satisfy their ideals, let the basket be expanded, including those aspirations that only a moment ago had no voice so as not to deform individuals, forcing them to choose something that does not represent their ambitions and ideals.

Our party is here to create opportunities for all and not to silence the voices of those who think differently from the majority or to alienate them by serving the predetermined interests of the privileged caste. Our motto is more opportunities for everyone, not the best opportunities for the few.

And just like an imaginary prison whose bars are melted away, so the fall of dictatorships or authoritarian regimes often leaves in a population, or the militants of a party led by such leaders, a state of limbo, weariness and helplessness, since the people at most had only the vaguest idea of what truly occurred during those years, for many had chosen comforting lies over bitter truths.

And when the prisons shatter, the 'ruling beast' crumbles and is appropriated by everyone's unconsciousness, and the only law is that of the jungle, where everyone's personal mirror convinces them that they are above everyone else. Therefore, the mirror where the 'goddess of justice' brushes her hair is neither the mirror of the 'ruling beast', as an absolute person who stands above everyone else nor that narcissistic personal mirror which lulls one into endless hibernation sleep.

The latter has happened to our country in recent decades. From the nothing that we were as individuals in the eyes of the state and the rulers in the previous dictatorial system, nowadays, we have already been metamorphosed into slumbering creatures, sleeping on a myriad of mirror fragments.

Therefore, we need democracy and free elections to shake us to the foundation from this futile lethargic sleep and to dismantle and fabricate the 'ruling beast', —again and again—whenever necessary, in keeping with the demands of the times, which adapts and flows with the gradual replacement of generations, and not according to the mindset of a man in his monkish cowl! ..."

And the crowd roared and burst into cheers, like the crest of a wave when it breaks into thousands of whitewater splashes as it crashes against the steep ridges of the rocks.

It is far more difficult to break the mould with goals you have set for yourself than to follow the evocative odour of the bazaar. And most people needed a guide, without which their lives would turn into indifferent slavery or a banshee's endless shriek. And in this way, they run after Mrs. Bekteshi's gentle redolent, like kids going to a dance party. In just the same spirit, full of joy, the blessed children, along with their parents, surrounded Mrs Bekteshi and whirled about her like a flywheel at the campaign's closing rally. They vied for her attention, hoping to build a silent bridge between them through the eyes — to steal, if they could, a smile. As they leapt towards her in laughter and delight, they marvelled aloud that this woman — whom they had once seen elevated high upon the proscenium of the theatre — now stood among them, made of flesh and blood, and not as a fleeting figment of a dream.

Everywhere, you saw people frenetically joining the tip of index fingers of each hand, with the tip of the thumb of the other, as therewith they made a rectangular frame fixing in the imagination Mrs. Bekteshi as she passed by.

She always held her rallies and pressed the out in the open, in a park or a stadium, since the arousing and the vitality that nature scattered and bestowed among the people before, during, and after the oration, she could not acquire in an indoor environment of any kind.

The bright rays of the sun, without which she could not do without, as well as every gust that stroked her face and ruffled the hair of everyone present, without exception, were the little things that made her feel one with the crowd, as a whole.

The atmosphere she conjured at her gatherings resembled the jubilant days when nations are liberated—whether from internal satraps or foreign puppet rulers.

But, while in the air, the dulled senses of the populace were beginning to sharpen, still the windmills of the institutions continued to spin a whirlwind of fear and monstrous panic, frightening and bewildering a significant portion of the public. It was a filthy game, where half of the species of those who were holding the reins of power exploited the opposition of a part of the population against anarchism to push them towards authoritarianism, which represented the other side of the same species. A game of table tennis, where the whole population, including themselves, served as the court, and although the players played worse as the match progressed, they thought themselves to be irreplaceable, forgetting that when a game bores the wide population, they will inevitably invent another one, rendering the existing caste of rulers into something totally ineffective and inferior.

Thus, the parties that represented the authority in power were a hybrid and silly mish-mash, where anarchy was preached at the base, while the authoritarianism of the enlightened and indisputable leader was hailed at the top of the party pyramid.

Mrs. Bekteshi was like a twinkling spark that fell from the sky, quietly biding her time until the gunpowder had fully dried—so that, with the fire of her pathos, she might reignite the dreams of ordinary people, now drifting aimlessly with a misaligned compass, jobless and futureless, haunting taverns and pubs like the living dead. For one becomes such a lifeless creature when dreams are dashed, and opportunities are sculpted and restricted according to the tastes and interests of a privileged few—whoever they may be—rather than shaped by the creative force of the soul and the will of each and every one.

In this way, the party and the political movement, inspired by Mrs. Bekteshi and Pasqualino and supported by many others who had sobered up and had realised the vile games played at their expense, still needed a miracle to shake the foundation of this caste of bureaucrats once and for all, who had long played and terrorized the people with a double-edged knife. And while the worshipers of the so-called "Holy Order", roaming with slavering slingshot, burst out creaking like a carnival firework, emitting piercing cries as soon as they appeared on a stage or a television programme, she, with her voice as clear as the cooing of a frightened dove hovered above the icy blocks of air, taking advantage of the warm winds rising from the bosom of the populace.

But, even though she had the charms now that allured a wider audience than she ever had as an actress, and, in all likelihood, she must have been walking on air about achieving the most important initiative in her life, she did not have that gleam in her eyes, as in the past after performing her role in a theatre play.

In the end, the more the crowd roared, the more a chill crept to the corners of her lips, slowly hardening into a stiff grimace. Behar, a past master in the work of hermit arts, noticed the change in her behaviour and drew closer to her. And while the ecstatic energy that the wave of the people exerted with increasingly more oppressive force against Mrs. Bekteshi along the campaign trail, on some occasions forcing her to address the crowd while gasping for breath, just as often Behar shook with a rumbling thunder of his voice, creating concentric centrifugal waves of sound, that rippled through the masses and pushed their unruly fervour back towards the edges.

"I think that the pureness of your thoughts expressed in your speech has refreshed the peoples' minds enough for tonight. After this, a hot bath will wash away any lingering unease or stray sorrows clinging to the honeycomb of your memory." Behar said to Mrs. Bekteshi with a sweet voice shortly after concluding the speech in order to ease her nerves, which were strained during the campaign trail.

"And God knows where I would be if, after the orations, I didn't rest my head on your shoulder. Maybe in a world where yesterday didn't happen, today doesn't exist, and tomorrow will never come." she replied with elegance, as was characteristic of her. And, even though those were pretty empty words, they nonetheless sounded appealing when she uttered them because of the subtle gestures of a hand passing through her hair, or the sudden change of facial expression or something else alike, as the case may be, with which she accompanied these statements.

"Maybe on Pasqualino's shoulder," says Behar, waiting for her reaction with ears pricked like a hound awaiting its quarry to fall after it has been shot.

"His shoulder is too smooth, and I'm afraid that my mind will slip and break off into thousands of fragmented memories. I am tired of feeling sorrow about the same thing over and over again. Grief multiplied is unbearable. Maybe my unconsciousness needs to clot this meaningless vein of futility in my heart once and for all and carve out a new path." she answered with a radiant smile, which would melt even the darkest recesses of the universe.

"Blocking an existing path might backfire, no matter how agonising and pointless it may be walking on it, without first cutting a new one." said Behar.

"Well, sometimes the ideal that guides us in life must burn to ashes everything inside us in order to blaze a new trail." Mrs. Bekteshi answered on the spot.

And while Behar was trying to conjure something up, a thunderous bang, like a cannon shot, made the ground under our feet roll and the window panes in the buildings around us wobble and break.

The crowd gathered in the square was briefly bewildered, but when that deafening blast was followed by fireworks at the close of the campaign, their ovations grew still hotter, with cheers vibrating through the buildings and echoing all over the city, just as it happens when raging bulls are chasing people on the streets in traditional Latin festivals.

At that moment, I saw fleetingly before my eyes the silhouette of Ilir in the middle of the throng of people. Since the last time we met, every night, chimeras carried me off in my sleep, shadow-passing me in the streets of the city. And as I walked, no matter where I would be, I always felt that I glimpsed his shade. At one time, I could spot Ilir among the crowd of pedestrians as we passed each other at a crosswalk. Another time, I took heed of his likeness in a reflection hovering over the window panes by the shops in the streets. Occasionally, I would catch sight of him on the beach, where people swarm during the end of summer and at other times during a rally that the various parties organized. And, every time I saw and followed him behind, trying to reach him, I noticed that he was chasing someone or something that crept along the walls like a shade. And, every moment I drew near him to attract his attention, I woke up. And this kept going on in a vicious circle, spotting Ilir again and again in different circumstances without the slightest association with the dream of the night before.

Surprisingly, just as he had appeared in my dreams of late, Ilir was accompanied by a tall, elderly, grey-haired man dressed in black. His small, pockmarked face was bounded by an almost round chin and a small pointy nose, which were insignificant in relation to the rest of his features. His freckly, liquid eyes, large as binocular lenses, were of green colour with a light brown tint and swapped colour and brightness according to the occasion, adapting to the environment, the surrounding lighting, and his mood. Sometimes transparent like two clear crystal springs, sometimes impenetrable like two ponds of water during the night, when the moonshine dances across the surface. The two of them seemed utterly delighted in each other's company, talking constantly and laughing themselves sick, so much so that passers-by glanced at them with disbelief, assuming they were either drunk or mad.

I decided to tail them to see where they would go. After ambling along the main boulevard, they headed towards Ilir's endz, and then I saw them enter the back door of his house. I did the same, and as I pulled the door handle to go inside the garden, I immediately noticed the marble block in the same place and condition as the last time Ilir was working on it. Now that I was looking at it more carefully, the features of a man were naturally impressed upon it. And, like the stone heads discovered in the jungles of Guatemala, that block of marble rested in a corner of the garden, almost covered by a lush vegetation, with its eyes looking up to the sky.

To my great surprise, the contours of the face, which were sculpted by nature itself, bore an uncanny resemblance to the old man with whom I saw Ilir walking as though his very head had been encased in a block of ice. While beside him stood a clay specimen of mould, according to which, apparently, Ilir had planed to model the block of marble the last time I'd seen him.

The old man, whom I neither knew nor had ever seen before, though I strongly suspected he was the very same who had placed the commission at the last Biennale, stood leaning against the marble block. Somehow, Ilir had decided not to work on the marble block anymore, and he with a brass bucket was pouring molten bronze and copper into the clay mould, which slowly came out and covered the statue like a figurine when you pour a jar of honey on it.

The clay mould, consequently, was gradually being transfigured into a statue of crimson colour. The sculpted features began to stand out sharply as the molten metals solidified. The light of the surrounding environment began to illuminate its surface. As far as I could see, this statue depicted the body of a man, which rose up from a molten pool of metal, the lower limbs being misshapen from the thigh down, and instead, ligatures hung like a stream of irregular lines, becoming one with the amorphous matter from which it sprang forth. The rest of his body was straining every nerve, slightly arching backwards in a semi-circle, like an athlete in mid-air clearing a crossbar in the high jump. But whereas the channels all strength into lifting his entire body weight over the crossbar successfully, the man in the clay model kept his left arm tucked tightly to his body while his right arm stretched in a backstroke. In the palm of his outstretched hand rested a baby, swaddled in woven wraps, clutching the man's thumb tightly with its tiny hand, that he was trying to push past the invisible crossbar. The tightly clenched jaws of the man, stretched at utmost in a semi-arched standstill, express unfathomable and countless pains and sufferings, which had etched their mark over the years on his soul and face. His thick eyebrows were somewhat furrowed and wavy, his eyes large, and his lips were tightly locked and twisted from overexertion. Indeed, it cannot be stated with certainty whether it was he who was trying to push the baby over the invisible crossbar or whether it was the infant who was pulling the man over it. There was so much concentration and tension in that arch of his body, as he was trying to leap beyond that invisible barrier blocking his jump that it seemed as if the point of gravity and attraction of the whole universe condensed on that singular point. As soon as the statue was cast in bronze, lightning flashed across its surface. Then came a deafening explosion—far louder than the bang that had marked the end of the campaign, and a mushroom-shaped cloud of smoke was seen to rise up high to the sky. Side by side with it, Ilir, together with his acquaintance, were lifted up in the air, the marble block and the bronze statue as well, until reaching a point where everything was blown up and turned to ashes. And, the fumes left behind, driven off by a gust, merged with the huge plume of smoke that was spreading evenly all over the sky, and particles of soot began to rain down on his garden, covering the greenery with a black mantle.

Early the next morning, after a sleepless night locked in my room as dark as he inside of a pocket, the day stirred to life as the soft rustle of an envelope slides beneath the door. I stand up with clumsy movements and, patting my bare feet on the floor, I approach the door and take the envelope in my hands.

In the sender's corner, in black letters, was the address of the prison where Besian had been transferred. I immediately tore it open nervously, with trembling hands troubled by a bad premonition because I had not long since visited Besian in detention.

After unfolding the scribbled sheet of handwriting, I began to read "My dear friend T.!

I'm trying to put in ink those words that my parched lips could not give voice to in the last meeting together.

Besides, when the iron enters your soul and eats you alive by cutting you off from the outside world, and the strings of dreams woven in freedom, while this alienating system that we call 'Justice' has turned you bellicose towards the people closest to your heart, running meticulously a 'divide and conquer' strategy, you have no choice but to wither away.

Here, the days glow like a thousand and one suns and then roll one by one into the solitude's loch, while the groans divaricate from the crack of my heart out of kindness.

Even though sometimes my soul shatters for a few moments out of this world, I do it only to look at Edlira's face again with revived eyes. Ah, as a love's young dream, do kisses precipitate, like a blustering wind that anticipates the hurricane, like a swirl that wants to immerse me in.

And, while I drape the umbra of solitude, like gasping rosaries, like bitterness with regrets, my imagination silhouettes Edlira as her memory gathers in my chest.

Every morning, she appears next to me in the bed with clear winter sky colour sheets. Graciously, she reaches out one hand, grazing the sleek skin of the tummy with her fingernails, and nimbly passes her palm to cover the navel where one thousand and one eyes yell.

Oh, how I love those rosy gams, contouring her half-arched knees and fine calves, with her manicured toes, which she wiggles incessantly as if her soles are languishingly walking on the hot desert sand.

Also, her everyday gales of laughter, from now on, will be usurped by the guffaws of the prison guards as they make the headcount check.

The so sweet sounds of the belly fiddle, which she strummed any time we gathered with our friends, will now be drowned out by the dry sound of the railings as the guards strike the prison bars with a baton when they rattle my cage.

I will no longer hear the fragile beats of the heart, as I lay my head on her breast. Instead, I will listen to the ticking of the clock in my cell, reminding me every minute of my barren existence.

Fragmented memories constantly collide in my soul, as when she used to caress and throw kisses at me as if by a sling, on my lips, chin, forehead and all over my face.

The cries of pleasure that her blood-soaked lips, the passion of love beseechingly air, I will not experience like before because even the most phreatic eruption would become frozen solid in the as cold as a witch kiss conjugal room.

No, I would never let the pyroclastic flow from her lip as our naked bodies roll on the love bed be replaced in my memory by the icy sighs inside that cursed den.

How many more mornings do I still have to spin her shadow, so that my soul may find rest?!

And how can I break this curse when the only thing I have are the bars of this damn cell as an exchange ring?!

Ahhh, Mother, I do hope you can forgive me for all the trouble I've caused you!"

A cold shiver ran down my spine the moment I put the piece of paper aside. It is the most shocking letter I have ever read, and I felt that each character and line was mentioned in the same breath as a farewell. My soul is burdened with sore and bleeding ominous thoughts, and as soon as I put on some clothes, I ran towards Besian's house to clear the murky waters of doubts that were lurking in my mind.

The weather is gloomy, and the clouds drift in the sky like plumes of tobacco smoke reflecting in a mirror.

As soon as I step out onto the street, a muddy and blob-raindrops start to fall like cannonballs on a battlefield. Small rivulets floods everywhere on the road's surface, like thin capillaries that were thirstily absorbed by the ditches and drainage canals of wells and waterways. The scorched ground gulped down every drop of tears that the sky pattered with moans this day.

My worst fears are realised as soon as I cross the threshold of the tenement, where wailing voices are echoing from Besian's flat. The stairs are seething with not a dry eye to be found on the faces of his relatives, friends and colleagues, so much so that I have to make my way through to his apartment. Once there, I hug his mother, who, dressed in black, is crying with sobs racking her body, fallen into a heap. The only words that I can put together from her stammering talk are "My darling, take me with you, where you now rest eternally. I won't bother you at all, but I'll just fix your tuft of hair and moisture your lips, whenever you're thirsty. My child, boy!" and she says all this to me as if her son is there in front of her, while she fastens my arm tightly with her hand, like an eagle's talon.

"I'm sorry, Mom, I'm so sorry... My heart aches with grief. Tell me, how may I... what is going on? How did it happen? How may I ease your pain?" I ask her piping my eye, already certain by now that my worst fears had become a reality.

But no, not at all! Besian's younger brother told me the uttermost calamity that had happened, who, parting me away from her hands, led me to the other room, where just by ourselves, he told me heart to heart that Besian and Edlira were dead.

Instantly, my knees gave out, and I would have fallen down if it hadn't been for his quick reaction to catch me and bring me to my senses.

A deadly silence hung over us, and as I got a grip of myself, he told me that they both had celebrated the sanctuary of their privacy with their last breaths.

Yesterday, during the family visit, Besian had not spoken a single word, not any different from the last time I saw him, but had simply stood ogling at each of his relatives with a blank expression on his face. Only later would they figure it out that it had been the anticipatory face of death, that which had strained every muscle of his face and body. At the end, before they parted, he had taken his mother's hand and kissed it, and two drops of hot tears had slipped from his eyelashes, just as he had the day he set out on the road to emigrate, wetting her lined hand.

After finger-combing his hair and fondling his smooth cheeks and his wrinkled forehead, she said, blubbering, that she would come back and see him again next week, and if there was anything that he needed, he should let her know so she could fetch it for him.

"The only thing I need from you is to smile whenever you think of me." Besian had told her and kissed her hand, which would be the last.

Once the meeting with their family had ended, Besian and Edlira spent the rest of the day in the conjugal visitation room. They, as if blindfolded, had executed a cunningly crafted plan in cold blood, drenching their clothes, bed sheets and themselves with water. And with a short wire, which Edlira had surreptitiously sneaked through the checkpoint without being noticed, disguising it as a hair bound, they had made an extension, dismantling the electrical outlet that was located above the head of the bed, and connected it to the plug... And thus, hugging each other tightly, they had let the electric current penetrate thoroughly into their soaked-to-the-bone bodies, turning them to ashes.

To ensure that there was no resolve to their eternal wedding vows, Besian had clenched the bare wires with his teeth so that due to the instinctive counter-reaction, the jaws would tighten the clasp even more, fatally conducting the deadly electric current. The last moans and gasps that were heard coming from the room were underestimated by the prison guards, who had thought it were the yelps, squawks and whooping of two lovers blowing off kinky steam.

As Besian's brother finished recounting the harrowing events, I collapsed into a nearby chair. I couldn't tell whether minutes, hours, or even days passed. All I remember is regaining consciousness as I am dragging my feet in the middle of a throng of people on the way back from the cemetery when Ikun gently lifts my hand and pulls me towards her. I don't know if she was more ravishing that night when we went together and visited Behar in the hospital or now that she is wearing a black taffeta dress that is somewhat tighter at the bottom and shows off her slender waist as never before. While on her head, she is wearing a round hat, also black in colour, and a veil with fine details, that drapes down over her shoulders and covers her eyes and face up to just above the lips.

It is a little past afternoon. On the way back, we stop at the house long enough to pull up the stakes that Ikun has already packed and then catch our breath at the port of the city D., boarding the ferry along the shores that are wet by the waves of the unruffled sea, as if they were the waves of a lake, those that were spuming majestically on its shores.

While drinking coffee in the ship's restaurant, I read in the newspaper that the election campaign was over and that the party led by Mrs. Bekteshi and Pasqualino had managed to reap a landslide victory. It also mentions that

Mrs. Bekteshi and her personal bodyguard had not been seen since that day, and I later learned that they were both rolling out the remaining days of their lounging beneath palm trees and sipping from coconuts after eloping to an island. Pasqualino was appointed Prime Minister, while the position of his deputy was held by Karl, who had previously pulled the pin from all his functions at the hotel.

Undoubtedly, what had turned the situation in their favour was the explosion at a military base. Along with it, many innocent people had been blown to pieces who worked there under slavish conditions, as well as a crowd of art lovers who were attending the inauguration of a statue nearby. This base had been turned into a factory, where ballot papers for the election were fabricated, which, as reported by a state agency, the blast was the result of a "technological accident" and so the election was forced to take place by blackballing, where manipulation was out of the question.

The pale autumn sun is swinging between the white Pileus cap peregrinator caravan of the thin threads of clouds, as the strings of a guitar, which the onshore breeze is blowing northward until at last they are gulped down by the sea. The golden rays are glittering by hundreds and thousands of waves, which, like sprightful dolphins, leap up and spindrift, still flickering its dim yellow beams, and then mirroring on my face, Ikun and her betrothed, who in the meantime is coping the squat on the bow, enjoying the seagulls and pigeons that have the courage to fly off the coast, feeding them with various grains.